Glitter

DIANA DeRICCI

PURPLE SWORD PUBLICATIONS

GLITTER
Copyright © 2013 DIANA DERICCI
ISBN 978-1-61292-076-4
ISBN 10: 1612920764
Cover Art Designed by Anastasia Rabiyah
Photographs Copyright wtamas, fotolia.com
Edited by Shoshana Hurwitz and and Traci Markou

Published by Purple Sword Publications, LLC
Tucson, Arizona, USA
www.PurpleSword.com

Dedication:

Glitter is for the readers who asked for Josh and Laurence's story. I hope they enchant you as much as they did me.

With a special thanks to my beta reader, J., who read Glitter as a trial by fire and did a superb job.

CHAPTER ONE

"OH, CHRIST. What's he doing here?" Josh growled in not too well hidden distaste.

Gregory lifted his head from his textbook, hunting their immediate vicinity of the outside commons. "Who?"

"The glow stick."

Gregory arched an eyebrow, peering now in the direction Josh meant. "Uh... You mean Laurence? Because I think RJ would kick your ass if you called him that."

Josh made a look of disgust and suddenly became engrossed in his studying as the men approached the table, though men was loosely used when it came to those two, one especially.

"Hey, guys. Guess who passed his final?" RJ announced.

"Congrats, man!" Gregory gave a beaming Laurence a high five.

The stretch of Laurence's arm bared a strip of stomach beneath the hiked lightweight white sweater. Josh blinked when he realized he'd been drawn to that flash of skin—*again*. He shivered, anger stiffening his spine. He was not into guys!

He slapped his book closed. "I have to go. Professor Stromburgh is too punctual to be late."

"Okay."

"Bye."

He didn't wait around to say more, or to see if a third voice joined the litany. With his pack tossed over his shoulder, he stomped into the crowd, and away from that table.

Fucking pricks. He snarled, but forced himself to calm down when he almost trampled a pair of girls turning a corner in his direction. It wasn't that he had a problem with gays, or lesbians, or dykes, or... Hell, whatever they wanted to be called.

He *did* have a problem with the way he couldn't seem to keep Laurence from getting to him. Josh was *not* gay.

And shit, Laurence was so gay, he glittered.

With the time it took to reach his class, he'd calmed enough to be able to listen with at least half an ear. Finals were in two days for him. He needed to concentrate.

Instead he doodled, and his mind wandered back to his first semester and the class—just the *one* class, thank God—that he'd shared with Laurence. Josh knew gay people, though he'd never been outwardly friendly to any before.

Laurence was the first time he'd truly been able to watch the infamous "twink" in the wild, its natural habitat. He remembered staring like Laurence was some sort of special attraction through most of the class. It was a sight Josh had never been exposed to back in Colorado.

He'd become fast friends with Gregory, and managed to avoid anything to do with Laurence that whole first semester. Then

Gregory met RJ, and while he was gay, he didn't discomfit Josh to the point of palm sterilization every thirty seconds. Like they'd been best buds their whole life, RJ and Laurence became an inseparable menace.

Josh let out a quiet breath, gazing around the room, alone in a crowd. No one was paying him the least bit of attention. Spotting the length of the final notes on the board, he tried to focus, but drifted again.

They'd made it through the summer and lo, no Laurence last fall. He'd almost rejoiced. Josh should have known better. Their schedules had been polar opposites, so even though RJ talked about him, Laurence was a person in absentia to Josh.

Gregory had started dating Rachel, and sometimes they double dated, himself with one of Rachel's girlfriends. Josh wasn't steady with anyone yet, and with summer coming again, he just wanted to get through his finals. His work load was going to increase his third year. He wanted to have some fun this summer to pad the days and weeks when he'd have no down time. He had a timeline, a plan, and nothing short of the apocalypse was going to keep him from meeting and exceeding his goals.

His parents had worked hard to get him this shot at a college education. He wasn't going to fuck it up by playing around.

"Hey, man, chill. Prof's eyeballing you, dude."

Josh stopped tapping his pen, unaware he'd been doing it. Sinking lower in his seat, he said out of the side of his mouth, "Thanks, Billy."

"No worries, bro. Fuck, I don't know if I can pass this one," Billy muttered. He scribbled furiously, holding his head in a palm, his face scrunched as he tried to make heads or tails of the techno-babble that Professor Stromburgh excelled at.

"It's just a tech course."

"Shove it, brainiac," Sally snipped over her shoulder from the seat in front of him. "You're the damned ace of this class. The rest of us peons have to actually, oh, I don't know, like study." She flipped back around with a huff, poring over the text in front of her in time with the monotone lecture.

Josh hunched into his seat, and did his best to become invisible. He also paid attention and took the notes.

GREGORY SAT next to Josh on the beach early that summer, both watching the nearly naked smorgasbord of female *come and get me* walk by. Josh was due for a three week summer break at his parents' and before he left, he found Gregory to hang out. He missed his family, but it was getting harder to leave behind everything he knew in LA too. The beach seemed like a no-brainer, a chance to hangout after finals.

Gregory tipped the water bottle back and drained it. "I'm thinking about asking Rachel to marry me."

Josh's mouth popped open. "No! I mean, man... No, I mean that. No!"

"What? Why?" Gregory raised his sunglasses, his eyes wide and a little distressed at Josh's outburst. "She's a good person. I love her, and she likes Mom."

"Gregory." Josh exhaled roughly. "It's been a little over a year. Give it some time."

Gregory tilted his head. "You think I'm rushing?"

Josh debated holding his tongue, then because he trusted Gregory like a brother and had Gregory's best interests at heart, told him, "Just wait until you graduate. Things may change."

Gregory sifted through the sand with his toes. "Yeah, you're probably right. There's no reason to rush before we even finish, huh?"

Relieved when his best friend didn't sound exactly put off with his opinion, he nodded. Gregory was young still, though a little older than Josh. He needed time to enjoy that. "Yeah. There's time. Besides, if you get hitched, who'll come slum with me on the beach?"

Gregory groaned, then laughed. "Moron." He leaned back on his elbows, elongating his frame next to where Josh sat. A knee tapped his upright shin. "Hey, Mom wants us to come to dinner Saturday. The usual end of term deal. You in?"

"Are you kidding?" Josh grinned, glad he hadn't upset Gregory. He didn't have many friends, still a little too much of the backwater kid from Colorado in a strange, wild land. "I would never pass up a dinner with Mickie and Ian. They're like having my folks here, only they don't nag."

"Great. I'll let her know to add you to RJ and Laurence, then."

What? "Laurence?" He kept himself from squeaking in shock. "RJ and Laurence will be there?"

"Yeah, the whole gang." Gregory distractedly watched a pair of long legs and the bikini-clad body they were attached to saunter by. "It'll be fun." Then he was up and jogging after that tan pair of legs.

"You, my friend, are a dog. That is why you shouldn't ask Rachel, not yet, anyway," Josh mused under his breath, just shaking his head at his friend's antics. He did his best to ignore the roll of his stomach at the mention of being in close quarters with Laurence the following weekend.

He'd survived another year, on target to get his degree. He'd decided he wanted to teach. Josh loved helping other students, and wanted to see them succeed, just like he was doing, the small-town farmer's son who'd made it to the west coast and college. Never since that tech class with Sally and Billy did he take a class for granted. Neither of them passed, and it bothered him. The material wasn't ultra difficult, but helping them both the following semester, he struck on something he hadn't known. He liked instructing, sharing, encouraging. Josh wanted to be the man with the answers, or the knowledge to find them. Watching others' expressions when they got to a solution was the best feeling in the world for him.

His father was proud of him, and hadn't been shy in suggesting he return home to teach at the high school. Josh wasn't sure that was where he wanted to end up, so he'd left it open.

Josh had also survived another year in close proximity to Laurence. The man was impossible. If they weren't arguing, Josh had to admit, they did laugh a lot. He'd grown a little more accustomed to, or maybe just desensitized to, his flamboyant nature. Though he'd almost had a seizure the day he'd whipped out a bright yellow feather boa in the library. Josh was positive they were going to get kicked out, but somehow they'd survived detection by the book police. His lips twisted at the memory. He hadn't laughed that hard in ages as Laurence pranced and batted lashes that were too long and thick for a guy. He'd said he was practicing for an upcoming part in a play, though Josh had his doubts. He really had a feeling that was just Laurence underneath his better refinements of civility.

Josh snorted, hooking his arms around a raised knee. Laurence was like that child's game, "pick the one that doesn't belong". With naturally nearly-platinum blond hair and crystal clear-as-the-sea blue eyes, he was pure California primate. Until he opened his mouth, or moved. The man was a walking sass-trip.

"You're in a better mood." Gregory plopped down beside him, startling Josh out of his thoughts. And he realized he *was* smiling.

"Just thinking."

"Well, don't hurt yourself."

"Prick."

Gregory just chuckled and stretched out on his stomach.

Josh's mind wandered again as another group of young women paraded by. God, it was like a free show on the beach. It was the closest to indecent exposure that he'd ever come to. His father would have a heart attack. Josh covered his mouth, hiding his snicker. There were some things his father just didn't have to know about his son's life in college.

JOSH RANG the Anders' doorbell, stuffing his hands into the deep pockets of his pants. One thing he missed about home—there was always some place to hide his hands in his jacket. He smiled at Mickie when she opened the door. He was no sooner in the door then he was engulfed in maternal arms for a welcome hug.

"God! You've grown."

"Mickie," he teased. "I'm twenty-two. I'm done growing."

She tilted her head, peering up at him with knowing brown eyes, just like Gregory's. "Look, I'm short. Cut me some slack."

"Yes, Ma'am." Josh gave her a strong hug in return.

"They're in the kitchen," she said, ushering him into the house with a wave in that general direction.

Josh really did adore Gregory's parents, but everyone that he knew who met them did. They were great, welcoming and supportive all the way around with Gregory's ragtag group of friends.

A loud laugh filled the house as he neared the kitchen.

Laurence. Even the insane ones.

Laurence had his back to him, talking to Gregory and his dad as he entered the kitchen, but it wasn't who was there that made Josh stop dead in his tracks.

It was something unexpected, and it didn't compute.

It was the jeans.

Josh was accustomed to seeing Laurence in anything from normal clothing to something outlandish, like a clubbing shirt that looked like a lion had used it to sharpen its claws. He'd thought Laurence was joking when he'd said he was actually *wearing* it out on a Friday night to go dancing with friends. The idea of Laurence showing that much skin had at once mystified and discombobulated him. There were things a man just couldn't take out of his make-up, and being small town and modest was apparently one of Josh's. He'd practically thrown a blanket over the other man, unable to breathe easier until he was gone and out of sight.

The jeans Laurence wore to dinner weren't even the shredded variety, so at first glance, Josh didn't understand why he'd been immobilized by them. No, the jeans Laurence wore were tight across his hips, painted like a second skin to the curve of his tight little butt. He was a lightweight man, but he wasn't stick skinny. The shape of his legs filled the jeans out smoothly. And after the cursory examination, Josh returned to the jut of a hip, the stance of his legs and couldn't help but think that Laurence was too sexy for his own good. Laurence was going to be shot like large game and mounted on some man's wall as a trophy if he kept dressing like that.

"Hey! You made it. RJ is like five minutes away." Gregory's voice snapped Josh back to the group in the kitchen.

Laurence whirled lightly on his toes and smiled warmly. "Hey, caveman."

"Fruit," Josh shot back out of habit. And with that familiar ground, the uneasy direction of his thoughts dispersed like a cloud before a hard breeze.

"Can't you kids play nice?" Ian admonished them, shaking his head at them both.

"That was nice!" Laurence piped up, little devils clearly visible on his shoulders as he grinned in Josh's direction. "You should hear him when I'm in shorts. Then he calls me Coconuts."

Josh groaned and leaped after Laurence. A squeal and sharp laughter echoed through the house as Josh chased him into the living room. Gregory leaned out of the path of escape, unscathed, but barely. The doorbell pealed and mayhem ensued as they charged in RJ's direction.

RJ was smart enough to duck and cover.

Josh caught Laurence and wrapped him in a bear hug. Held off the floor, Laurence's sneakers kicked the air in front of them, unable to fight Josh's larger size or strength.

"Uncle!" Laurence gasped, laughing loud and hard.

"Put him down," Mickie scolded coming up behind them. "Boys. You never grow up."

"Physical hazard," RJ blithely pointed out, sidling past the wrestling pair to not be part of the fallout.

"It's Josh. He can't keep his hands off me," Laurence purred, going limp in his arms.

Josh let Laurence go so fast, he almost fell on his ass.

"Hey!" Laurence shouted, managing to not become one with the floor at the last second.

Josh tossed his hands up, backing away. "Wasn't me," he called out.

"Dude, wasn't me hasn't lived here in over ten years. Give it up." Gregory gave him a swat on the back of the head in addition to the warning.

"Dinner!"

"Saved by the mom," Josh groused, brushing passed an indignant Laurence.

The phantom press of a caressing hand slid down his ass as he strode by, and Josh whirled, glaring.

"Wasn't me," Laurence parroted, grinning like an innocent angel.

Josh lowered to growl into Laurence's ear. "It's on, glow stick."

"Ooh!" Laurence cooed, his mouth tipping up at the corners. Taunting mirth and secrets darkened his eyes. "Do I get to pick out the china?"

Josh was yanked away by strong arms before he throttled Laurence as an appetizer.

CHAPTER TWO

GREGORY TURNED the key to start his car, pulling away from his parents' home a moment later. The house shrunk then vanished when they turned a corner. Laurence hated seeing the evening end. He always had a great time talking about the latest movies with Mickie.

Gregory shook his head at Laurence. "Why do you push him like that?"

Laurence slid a hand through his hair, shaking it loose to let it fall again to his shoulders. "Because it's so easy. He practically flinches around me and RJ. He's homophobic."

Gregory didn't reply right away.

Uh huh. 'Cause I'm right, Laurence gloated in silence.

"He's not. He's come around since I first met him."

Laurence shrugged. "Just because he deigns to talk to me, doesn't mean he likes me, gets me or anything. He certainly doesn't approve."

"Since when have you needed approval?" Gregory asked in pure disbelief.

"There's only a year left, then he'll go on his merry little way," Laurence danced his fingers through the air, ignoring the question, "and leave us all alone. He hasn't liked me from day one. I can't help that he's an asshole." Laurence gave Gregory's profile a meaningful glare. "He only tolerates me because we're friends. He'd as soon see both me and RJ vaporized."

Gregory's expression darkened. "Not cool. He's not like that, I swear."

"Gregory." Laurence sighed through a heartfelt groan. "He is every bit like that. He wasn't flirting earlier. That man is an ox and doesn't know his own strength!" Laurence folded his arms over his chest, restraining from rubbing where Josh had held him like a damned vice. It was bad enough Laurence felt like a midget next to Josh, he didn't have to be thrown around like a sack of potatoes on top of it!

"It's not like he hates you—"

"Ah! But he does," Laurence stated. Seeing the growing scowl on Gregory's face, Laurence relented, but only a little. "Okay, maybe not *hate*. I'll give you that, but there's disdain, disgust, belittlement. I'm an English major. Want me to keep going?"

Gregory slouched into the driver's seat. "Okay, okay. He's a guy from rural bum-fuck. You're a species he's not accustomed to. It doesn't mean you have to ride him—" Gregory completely ignored Laurence's guffawed snicker— "just to rile him up." Gregory slid a sideways look to Laurence. "You know you don't play fair to begin with."

"What are you talking about?" Laurence huffed.

Gregory arched an eyebrow. "You could have dressed for dinner, not clubbing."

Laurence let out an indignant squawk.

"Every time you know he's going to be around, you wear something outrageous."

Laurence took in his shirt and jeans. Even his sneakers were normal. Boring, but normal. "I don't see a problem."

"It's like you're taunting him, Laurence," Gregory pointed out coolly. "And you have since you two first met. Three years of it is enough."

Wide-eyed, Laurence twisted to gape at Gregory. Flashing lights of a passing car highlighted Gregory's features, firm and making a stand.

"What is this about, Gregory? I do not act any differently around or *for* him as I do anyone else."

Gregory wagged a finger at him and Laurence knocked it out of his face. "But you do. It's like you try to see how far you can go, how much it will take to shock him. Look, we're interning starting next semester. Just cut him some slack, okay? Josh is friends with all of us."

Laurence would have argued that more but there wasn't a real point to it. Josh Daily *tolerated* Laurence, RJ and their friends. Laurence had tried to be friendly with Josh. When they'd first met, he'd even thought he was something akin to scrumptious eye-candy.

The guy had come from Colorado, working beside his father on a small ranch. His hands were covered in scars from stringing fence and rough farm work, and he was broad as well as tall. In truth, the man *was* an ox, and he was a hot one.

Except that mental image vanished quickly under the light of day, because it hadn't taken long for Laurence to understand the type of man Josh was inside. He couldn't count the number of times Josh had rushed in the other direction when Laurence showed up. If he hadn't understood exactly *why*, Laurence would have been deeply offended. Unfortunately, Josh's reactions were almost laughable. And ultimately, sad.

Laurence didn't hide who he was. Why should he? No one told the cheerleaders not to be hyper. No one frowned and told the Goth kids not to wear black. And he had yet to hear a single person tell a redhead to dye their hair.

Why should Laurence be ashamed of who he was? There wasn't any way he was going to do that again, ever. He'd faced enough ridicule and criticism in high school, and he hadn't even been fully out there. He'd never even tried to kiss anyone from his school. College took care of that hole in his education as well.

He said goodbye to Gregory when he dropped Laurence off at his small apartment. It was a house that had been divided and remodeled into four efficiency apartments. Nothing worth *Good Housekeeping*'s stamp of approval, but it was in a good location near the college and not overpriced. Hearing a Cuban beat float down the narrow hall, he swayed his hips in time with the rhythm as he neared his doorway. His was on the second floor. Laurence loved his neighbors. Jeff was a wicked artist, and Samantha, his latest—and longest to date—girlfriend, was a dentist tech. At least half the couple was sane, he thought chuckling as he unlocked his door. He did a little hop-step to the music then sashayed into his place.

LAURENCE LOOKED up from his studies when Gregory pushed open the doors to the research archives. The room was clean, but a lot of other areas of the college were decorated for Halloween, and behind Gregory in the hall, someone cackled like a witch. They did a good enough job to shoot a shiver down Laurence's spine.

As the door closed, Josh trailed Gregory into the room. Laurence instinctively wanted to shrink down into his chair. Man, Laurence wished RJ was there, but he hadn't returned this fall. At least with RJ around, there was a buffer between himself and Josh. No such luck any longer.

RJ had fallen into some financial problems, something that had to do with his estranged mother. No matter how hard he dug, RJ wasn't telling. They still talked and hung out, but RJ had to drop out and was even then trying to get a small business started so he could support himself.

Sitting alone by a window, neither Gregory nor Josh spotted him as they walked into the room. Their lowered conversation was pretty easy to catch in the acoustic quiet.

"I don't understand, Josh." Gregory tugged out a chair and without looking around him, sat. "We've been together for two years and suddenly, she's 'I'm leaving after graduation'. What the fuck is that?"

Laurence blinked and sat up. *Oh, hell. Rachel.* He gathered his things, then stood and approached the table. "Hi guys," he said in hesitant greeting.

"Hey, Laurence."

Josh gave him a look and grunted. Laurence kept himself from rolling his eyes. This wasn't about Josh. For once. He studiously ignored the other man at the table.

Laurence slid out a chair across from Gregory. "Talk, sweetie. What happened?"

"She dumped me." Gregory gazed to nowhere. "Said she had a job offer in Sacramento after graduation, and she was going to take it. No questions asked. No discussion."

"The junior partnership she's been working on?" Laurence asked. Rachel was doing something law. It was more than he'd ever cared to know about the woman.

Gregory nodded, his trembling hands balled into fists together on the table in front of him. Lashes lifted to expose damp eyes. "I was going to ask her to marry me at the end of the term. And now..." His head sagged forward and he drew a hard, shaky breath. "It was like I was just a diversion, Laurence," he managed, dry and choked.

"And she broke your heart." Laurence reached across the table and covered his fists. "Women are evil."

Josh raised his eyebrows, but for once didn't make a cutting response. His silence didn't last.

"Not all of them," Josh finally interjected, though under his breath. Laurence couldn't have cared less and Gregory wouldn't believe him.

"Let's go get a drink somewhere, huh?" Laurence cajoled, rocking Gregory's hands.

"I have translations due." Gregory tried to make a responsible argument, but Laurence heard the lack of real conviction.

"It'll be here on Monday, sweetie."

"He's right." Josh added his support. "You need to get out of here." He stood from the table. "Come on. It's been a while since we've all gone out."

"RJ too?" Laurence asked, waiting for Josh to throw a fit.

"Sure. Call him. See what he's been up to," Josh said. Laurence hid his shock. Josh's answer proved he was willing to do what was needed to help their friend. For once, they agreed. The sky was going to fall.

Gregory got to his feet and just stood there, his hands slack at his sides.

Laurence curled an arm around Gregory's waist and Josh threw one over his shoulders. "Let's go make some friends with the porcelain gods," Josh said with sympathy.

Josh drove them all to a bar not too far from the campus. Laurence called RJ on

Gregory's cell phone and gave directions where to meet them. "He'll be here in about an hour," he informed them when he was done talking.

Gregory sat in numb silence not replying, but Josh gave him a tight nod in the rearview mirror.

The three of them walked in the front doors of the club and found a place. The drinks started flowing. Laurence kept an eye on Gregory, noting he really wasn't caring what he had in his hand and that worried him. This wasn't normal for Gregory.

Eventually, RJ's disgusted voice twisted Laurence around. "Good God. I guess since I'm the last one here, I'm the driver," he remarked, sweeping a hand at the field of downed bottles and empty glasses on the table. "Did any of you eat anything?"

"Nope!" Laurence chirped. He was leaning heavily into Josh, simply because he was the one sitting next to him and the other side was empty. Not an option to lean that way. At one point, he had been boogying to the music, though he couldn't remember when he'd stopped. He'd never turn down good music.

"Hi, RJ." Gregory waved a bottle at him. "Come and join the party." He tipped the bottle in his hand to his lips and drained it in defiant punctuation.

"I would except I think I'm the only way you guys are getting home tonight," he groused, sitting down next to Gregory. "So what's going on?"

"Rachel broke Gregory's heart!" Laurence crowed over the blaring music. "Like an old shoe, she tossed him."

Gregory growled, scowling at him. "Not helping, Laurence."

Contrite, he reached across the table and patted Gregory's shoulder. "I'm sorry, sweetie. I am. I know you cared for her." Even if he didn't understand it, he could sympathize.

"I hadn't bought it, but I had the ring already picked out," Gregory mumbled. Glancing up, he added, "I need another beer." He waved his hand and a waitress homed in on their table.

"Okay, last round, guys. I'll get you home, but I don't want you puking in my car, either."

Laurence bent to rest right in front of Josh's torso. "It'll be okay, Gregory."

Josh swung an arm over Laurence's shoulders. The heat was comforting, holding him close. He curled under the weight until Josh spoke again. "Glow stick is right, man." Laurence stiffened, then shoved Josh's arm free. *Bastard*. He was Gregory's friend, not Laurence's even if they'd been mostly in agreement for the evening to help their friend.

Josh chugged his own beer without commenting, adding his request to the new order.

Watching them, Laurence figured it wouldn't hurt to have one more than one less. "One more for me too." Though his wasn't beer. He couldn't drink the stuff. A civilized man wouldn't dare. He stifled the giggle before it leaked free. He wasn't that toasted.

Watching the sway of the lights and wishing he was dancing made him reconsider that opinion. If they were at a gay club, he would be mixed into that gyrating mob without hesitation. Maybe finding some hot god to share a little time with. The fact that he was even considering it here proved he was pretty shot. He bounced and jiggled to the bass beat instead. Man, he wanted to dance. When he drank, he danced.

Okay, he was drunk.

He let out a dejected sigh and squished himself into Josh again.

JOSH TRAILED Laurence with his gaze as he shimmied through the crowd for the john. He squinted, then realized the man was *dancing* his way across the floor. The sway of the man's hips was hypnotic.

"Christ. Why does he wear those jeans?" Josh moved his tongue, ready for that next beer. He was hot and needed something to cool him down.

RJ twisted to see what he was complaining about. Gregory didn't move, hadn't moved much at all since they got there.

"What are you talking about?" RJ asked, playing with his keys in his hands.

"Those jeans are painted on. He's going to get mugged, or something." Josh wrapped his hand around the beer when it appeared in front of him. Those jeans always made Josh cringe.

"Don't worry, he can handle himself. He's small but he's not a wuss."

Josh wasn't so sure of that. Laurence weighed next to nothing. He knew it for a fact. He finished his beer and so did Gregory, and Laurence hadn't returned. Gregory didn't slow down, raising his hand to order again with Laurence MIA.

"Gregory," RJ tried, with little success.

"Fuck off, RJ," he snarled.

RJ bent close, tapping the table with a stiff finger. "Look, I'm here—"

"And you're taking me home. When I can't remember why I'm here," he finished, waving his beer when the waitress had their table in her sights.

"Fuck," RJ muttered. He plowed a hand through his hair, settling onto the seat for a long stay. "Cranberry and Sprite, please."

The waitress nodded. "DD drinks are on the house."

"Then set me up, sweetheart," he told her while tossing his keys on the table. She twirled and left, vanishing in the deepening throng of partiers who'd taken over the club as the night grew later.

Josh waited about another five minutes before real worry began to eat at him. When the waitress returned before Laurence, he slid from his spot. He didn't remember shoving people out of his way, or even if anyone tried to stop him.

The music grew louder the deeper he waded into the pool of swaying bodies. A few women tried to grab at him, but he brushed them off. A nugget of worry was morphing into something harder, fear almost, because

Laurence had conquered this same path, but hadn't returned yet.

And he was prettier than a lot of the women currently attempting to get Josh's attention. Josh wasn't stupid. He knew others would take that as a free pass to do some serious damage to Laurence. He'd gained a wholly different type of education since coming to California, and none of it was learned from a textbook. Laurence was tough, he'd give him that, but he wasn't superhuman. Josh still couldn't see him coming in his direction.

When he pressed on the bathroom door, it resisted, like someone was leaning on it from the inside. Josh snarled. Planting a shoulder against the wood, he shoved with his weight behind him and the door gave with an *oomph* clearly heard.

He was just in time to see Laurence kneeing a guy in the crotch. An upward cut didn't pack much behind it, but it stunned the guy in front of Laurence long enough to be able to sweep his assailant off his feet. The guy went down with a howled cry. Then the guy who'd held the door shut dove across the cramped space for Laurence.

That got Josh moving. He launched for the guy rushing Laurence, slamming him into a stone wall, face first. "Fucker," he growled into an ear. He smacked his head into the wall one more time then let him slither to the floor.

Laurence hopped over the man groaning on the floor holding his nuts. Josh backed up, a hand held out to steady him if he needed it. "You okay?"

"I'll live." Laurence raised a hand to his head and that was when Josh saw the marks on his face and throat.

Locking on those bruises and scratches, he saw red. Felt a rage that was close to boiling over in nothing flat. An anger that coiled and twisted, looking for anyone to strike out at. And for the first time ever in his life, he wanted to curl around the smaller man and protect him, not just from being beaten in the bathroom, but *protect him*. And maybe beat the shit out of the guys on the floor one more time just to make sure they didn't forget and tried to mess with the wrong guy again.

His stomach threatened to heave as confusion swamped him.

"Shouldn't fight on an empty, drunk stomach," Laurence muttered, weaving on his feet. He steadied himself with a hand on the sink edge for a few seconds, then once he was steadier, sashayed to the door. Josh ate up every little twitch of Laurence's cute butt. He shook himself out of his stupor in time to see the door start to close behind Laurence.

Stunned silent at the confusing morass of emotions, Josh followed Laurence out of the restroom.

CHAPTER THREE

LAURENCE PUT ice on his lip. "I'm fine." *For the thousandth time.* He glared at a growly Josh. "You didn't have to bring me home."

"Do you have something to drink?" Josh stalked to the kitchenette, ignoring Laurence's complaints.

"I have tequila, vodka, and I think some margarita mix. Check the cabinets," he replied, cross. He was sure he had more, but he couldn't think at the moment. Ever since Josh had stormed the bathroom like some avenger, he'd barely been able to breathe. He'd never seen Josh look so fierce, or hot. Not what he wanted to have his mind snagging onto. Plastered drunk sounded a whole lot better at the moment.

Josh had trailed him to the table like a second shadow and before he could sit down, told RJ and Gregory he was taking Laurence home, and of course, why. RJ had grown pissed. Not that Laurence blamed him. He didn't want to go home with Josh either.

Wrong.

He'd been furious that someone would dare attack Laurence, in the damned bathroom of all places.

"Humanity makes me sick sometimes," RJ bitched. "Take him home Josh. I've got Gregory."

"But I haven't finished my drink!" Laurence wailed, reaching for the tumbler, wanting to just sit and suck that down.

"We're done," Josh stated, accepting no arguments. With a hand on Laurence's arm, he dragged him outside and whistled for a cab.

"What about your car?"

"I'll get it later," he replied, opening the door to the first cab that hit the curb in front of them.

Laurence yanked his arm free. "Fine. But I'm going under duress."

"Sure, sure." Josh gave the taxi driver Laurence's address and they left the club, Gregory and RJ behind.

"Here." A filled glass of something— probably orange juice and vodka—waited in front of him, disrupting his internal bitch-fest. He set the small wrapped bag of ice on his leg and clasped the drink. "Don't worry. It's more juice than alcohol. I think we're done getting drunk." He sank down beside Laurence, a similar glass in his own hand. "What happened?"

Laurence took a sip, placing it on the table in front of him, to rest against the couch, wanting to only put the last hour or so behind him. "I went to piss, and was followed. It's what usually happens."

Josh's black eyebrows shot up. "Usually?"

Laurence flicked Josh's closest ear with a finger. "Problems hearing? Yes. It's why I learned how to defend myself." He palmed the ice and settled it to his lip again. "Though it's been a while."

Laurence skittered away a few inches when Josh's gaze turned thunderous.

"It's not like I *ask* for this shit to happen," he snapped.

Josh put a hand on his thigh and Laurence stiffened. And shut up. Josh was just like everyone else. *I'm gay, so of course I'm asking for it.* Laurence tried to slide away, out from underneath that weighted palm but Josh wouldn't let go.

"Why?" It was a menacing growl and Laurence tried not to flinch. He almost succeeded. Josh tilted to stare at him, his gray eyes even darker than they usually were.

"Why what?" Laurence fisted the ice bag, holding it, keeping himself from clobbering the caveman glaring at him. "Or do you mean how? Like how I tempt men into being utter assholes and into taking their fear out on me? Or how, just by not being ashamed to walk down the street like a human being, I offend people because I breathe the same fucking air?" Laurence was building steam, and getting angrier by the second.

"No!" Josh smacked his glass down. "Why do they want to hurt you?" He gripped Laurence's upper arms. "Why?"

Laurence gaped at him. *Shit. He just doesn't get it.* "Because I'm gay!"

"So?"

Laurence's mouth fell open. Utterly and wide. "You're kidding, right? You can't stand me yourself. You should be the first to understand dicks like that."

"What? You're full of shit." He stared at Laurence like he'd lost all his marbles, uncomprehending. Josh hadn't let go of Laurence, either.

"Please," he retorted in sheer disdain. To prove his point, he said, "In fact, you're touching me. Better let go or you're going to get gay germs."

Josh released Laurence so fast he hit sideways into the back of the couch.

"Get out," Laurence bit through a tight jaw, ignoring the twinge of pain the pressure caused. Just when he thought Josh could be human, he had to prove Laurence wrong.

Josh's eyes had gone wide, his hands held out. "No. It's not—"

"Just get the fuck out, Josh!" Laurence lurched from the couch and the sudden movement made his head feel like it was going to float away. He swayed. The ice bag fell from unresponsive fingers. The night was catching up to him with a vengeance. The room spun and a sense of weightlessness clouded his thoughts.

Oh, fuck. Then the world went black.

JOSH LEAPED to his feet and caught him just as Laurence's body went limp, saving him from cracking his head on furniture. Scooped against his body, Laurence snored.

"Now that's attractive," Josh mocked, though glad Laurence wasn't aware to hear him. He'd kill Josh. He eased away from the couch and table then strode into Laurence's bedroom. The apartment wasn't large to begin with, so finding the bed wasn't hard.

He eased Laurence's slack body onto the rumpled covers of the small bed. Josh's arms and hands were warm and tingled from holding Laurence so close. His heart pounded with a staccato beat as he fought against the waves of feeling he didn't understand. A lot of those feelings had to do with the rush of rage he'd been hit by when he'd interrupted the attack on Laurence. Something he hadn't ever felt or experienced had engulfed him in those seconds. He was still mired in many of them.

Josh sat beside him on the edge of the bed. With tender fingers, he stroked over the bruise on Laurence's jaw. In silence, he shook his head, his thoughts a larger mess than a chalk drawing in the rain.

"You have it all wrong," he breathed. "I don't care that you're gay. Not anymore." He tacked that on for good measure, to say it out loud, because it was true. After nearly four years as his friend, Josh knew he had changed, but what scared him was he wasn't finished with those changes. At least he didn't think he was. It didn't feel like he was. He swallowed. It more than scared him. It terrified him.

Josh had never gone looking for another friend who may have been in trouble. Had never felt ready to break bones like he had when he found Laurence pinned and being beaten against the bathroom wall.

He swept blond hair away from Laurence's features. Smooth, soft skin, that was now, unfortunately, marked with bruises. A not too long or narrow nose. Eyes, that if they'd belonged to a woman, he'd have gone so far as to call them beautiful, crystalline blue with thick and long, very pale lashes. And there was always Laurence's sass mouth. There was usually something outrageous being spewed out of it. But when there wasn't... No woman he knew had one as sexy as Laurence's when he smiled. Josh lifted his thumb and barely, so very hesitantly, skipped over Laurence's lower lip. His breath caught as a shock careened up his arm.

"You're too damned pretty to be a guy," he groused hollowly. Shivers crawled over his skin, and he ached, a definitive throbbing in his groin. A problem he'd learned to deny and ignore over the last few years, but feared he wouldn't be able to forever. Now that he knew what it was that had plagued him for so long and the one person—the *one* man—responsible for it. Josh had no idea how to deal with it. "That is what gets to me Laurence. But you're a guy, and I think I want you." He let out a terse breath. *So what does that make me?*

"SO WHAT are you doing after graduation?" Gregory grabbed his burger lunch from the fast food counter and found a booth to sit. Josh trailed after him.

Josh rolled his shoulders in his light jacket. Winter was fading, but he still felt more comfortable with a second layer. "Finish the internship and go home, I guess. Dad really wants me to go apply at the high school. Be closer to home."

"Your mom misses you, huh?" Gregory asked with a knowing smile.

"That's being kind," he remarked, stuffing a straw into his soda. "What about you?"

"I had an extension approved. I'm here for another two years, then we'll see."

"Congrats."

"I'm not complaining. The freelance work is starting to pick up."

Josh packed hot fries into his mouth. "Extra money, right?"

"Oh, yeah." Gregory grinned huge. "With Professor Knight's recommendations, I'm getting requests for translations and other work."

"Dude. You totally earn that though." Josh sat, blinking at Gregory who was hiding, eating his food. *Too modest.* "How many languages did you ace?"

"Four, five, something," he replied, ducking to hide his features. Gregory had always been humble about his linguistics ability.

They ate in silence for a few minutes, then, "Rachel is dating someone." Out of the blue.

Josh paused in his eating, swallowing thickly. He studied Gregory, but there wasn't anything there. The man was hiding it if knowing she was moving on hurt him. "And?"

Gregory held his burger aloft, boring into it with all of his attention. "I wished her luck."

"You'll find someone, man."

Gregory shrugged. "Not sure I really care anymore, Josh." Gregory took a bite of his food, signaling it was over for discussion. Josh didn't push it any further.

Rachel had done a number on Gregory, ripped him inside out. Josh didn't want her to suffer, he wasn't like that, but Josh really hoped his best friend found someone who made him happy. He also knew Gregory wasn't in any frame of mind to find her.

LAURENCE NUDGED the archives door open with a hip, propping it with the tip of his sneakered toes late on a Friday afternoon. He held a week's worth of study materials in his arms and needed to return them before the end of the day.

"Hold on."

Laurence startled when the stack of books was snatched from his arms and the door was easily opened. He turned and nearly swallowed his tongue.

Holy shit. Josh is smiling at me. When did Hell freeze over? He shook himself. He hated how much his body liked that smile. "Thanks."

"No problem. What are you doing here this late?" Josh waited and Laurence went in first. The door slid closed with a sibilant hiss.

"Had some work materials to return from Professor Stranton."

"Oh, right. Your mentor thing. How's that going?"

Laurence stood still just inside the door, shocked into mild silence that Josh knew anything about it. Since the night Gregory had tried to float his liver, they hadn't really spoken. He barely remembered much of it himself. He knew he'd been attacked, and had managed to leave mostly unscathed. A lot of it was fuzzy when it came to how he got home, though he knew Josh had been there. All he really could remember after that was Josh had pissed him off.

He'd awakened in his bed, still dressed, with a sore jaw. Though somehow, he'd kicked off his shoes and had wrapped a blanket over himself. Drunk. Then there were flashes of the argument he and Josh had been in the middle of, though it was distorted.

"It's going good, actually," Laurence finally got himself to say. "Stranton said she was very impressed with my ability to take the time help the lower classmen understand the lessons. She said patience is one of the hardest skills, and I can easily believe her."

"It's a good feeling, isn't it?" Josh turned with a nonchalant ease and strolled to the shelves where the books and texts he'd carried needed to go. Laurence followed, though he didn't have to point out where they went. Josh didn't even need a step to put them up. "I love teaching just because of that very feeling."

"Really?"

"Is it that surprising?" he asked calmly, an arched eyebrow his only exclamation.

Laurence was having a hard time comprehending. This had to be the longest conversation he and Josh had held the entire time they'd known each other. And it actually had meaning.

"Well, no," Laurence finally answered. "I just..." He stopped himself before he said something so totally wrong.

Josh smirked. "Just hadn't expected it of me?" he offered.

Laurence stuffed his hands into his back pockets. "Yeah, something like that."

"There's a lot you don't know about me Laurence." He motioned a hand forward. "Let's go for a walk."

"Sure you won't mind being seen with an out gay man?" It would be hard to talk with him running away.

Josh frowned. "That's one of things we need to clear the air on. It's long overdue." He stepped out from between the shelves. "Coming?"

"Sure," Laurence answered. *Though I'm obviously going around the bend to be thinking what I am about you.*

Laurence shut that little voice in his head up. Then for extra security, stuffed it behind a mental door and shoved a chair under the doorknob. Josh waited for him in the hallway outside the archives, holding the door to let him out of the room and Laurence gave him a speculative once over.

"Okay, who are you and what did you do with the caveman?"

Josh chuckled, a low rumble that unexpectedly warmed parts of Laurence on the inside.

"Come on, glow stick. Let's go walk outside."

Laurence smiled. "That's more like it." Territory he knew. This nicer version of Josh was throwing him off center. He'd known Josh for most of four years and only in the very beginning had he thought he was hot, or sexy.

Okay, so he'd always had some of those qualities. He could privately give him that. Laurence would never begrudge a man what God gave him, and he wasn't above looking. At well over six feet, Josh made Laurence feel absolutely tiny in comparison, and he wasn't. He was an average height and weight. Wavy, thick and luscious deep brown-espresso hair made Josh's dark thunderhead gray eyes even more stunning, and because of his darker coloring, he was almost always sporting a five o'clock shadow. Laurence had never seen, but he'd bet he had a delectable chest as well. But this...kindness wasn't the man Laurence knew. *A leopard can't change his spots.* He'd better remember that.

They walked in silence until they were on the sidewalk and clearing distance to get to one of the closer green spaces around the college. Trees were thickening again with spring leaves, and there was a scent of flowers on the air. Even the occasional breeze danced through the campus, bringing the allure of spring with it, heralding a warm summer. Laurence had absolutely no complaints about spring and summer in LA.

"I'm sorry."

Laurence tripped. Josh flung out an arm and caught him. Laurence would swear on a Bible if he had to that he did *not* just stumble. Laurence's fingers held on with a death grip to the strong forearm in front of him, leaving red marks as he managed to not face plant on the pavement.

"You okay?"

Laurence gulped. "Yeah. Uneven sidewalk," he replied breathlessly. Shaking at his knees, he forced himself to take steadier steps. "Thanks. Okay. Sorry about what?"

Josh let him go, though it felt remarkably slow, almost reluctant.

"Do you remember the last argument we had?"

"No, not really. We've had hundreds." Laurence couldn't pick just one.

Josh smiled, though it was tinged with sadness. "Yeah. My fault again. There is absolutely nothing wrong with you, and I'm sorry if I ever made you feel, you know..." He waved a hand in the air.

"Like a freak? Wait." Laurence stopped walking and crossed his arms, pressing his weight to a thrust hip. Was this about the night Gregory was dumped by Rachel? That had been last Halloween, the last notable and bad argument that he could remember. Those damned foggy memories. He'd shouted at him... He dug hard into those snips of memory. "Something about gay germs, and you?" *Was that it?*

Josh looked positively remorseful. "Yeah. I reacted wrong and hurt you, when you'd

40

already been beaten to a pulp. You didn't deserve it. I'm sorry." Josh lifted jet black lashes, exposing softened gray orbs.

That one look made Laurence feel soft and gooey inside. He did his best to firm his walls again, but they still wobbled.

"I've been trying to think of how to apologize. You said something that night and I couldn't understand it then why you thought..." He stopped and leaned with a tree at his back. He regarded Laurence with a very contemplative stare. "You think I hate you."

"Don't you? You've never been fond of me."

Josh looked out and away, his hands deep into his pockets. Laurence knew it was a habit of his when he was feeling vulnerable to hide his hands because of the scratch scars.

So what was making Josh feel like that now?

"I didn't understand you, but I think I'm starting to. We are friends, Laurence. If you needed me, I'd be there for you, just like for Gregory, and yes, even for RJ. It doesn't matter to me that you're gay." He lifted a hand when Laurence had a strong rebuttal for that. "People change, Laurence. You act in ways I'd never seen, but it's just who you are. I know that now." He met Laurence's wide eyes, a genuine smile flickering over full lips. "You're actually pretty funny, and cute, for a guy."

"Did you just say you think I'm cute?" He stretched upward and pressed a flat palm to Josh's forehead. "You must be dying." He smiled in jest to hide the wash of heat those few words shot through him. Heat that he'd always considered unattainable, because the man who created it inside him was the last person on earth to want Laurence.

Josh shoved him away, gently, laughing with him. "Hey, I'm not an insecure freshman. I can appreciate a hot guy, as much as a sexy woman."

Laurence examined him from head to foot. "You're serious?"

Josh nodded, that same playful smile teasing over his lips. Lips that held a sensuous appeal, one that Laurence could no longer ignore. He held the rush of awareness in check. He knew better, but he could accept Josh's olive branch.

"Wow," Laurence breathed in wonder. *Leopard? Meet your new coat.*

CHAPTER FOUR

ANOTHER SEMESTER was nearly done and graduation loomed. Josh was stuck on trying to decide what to do next. Stay and work further on his Assistant position, possibly getting another degree to take a teaching position for himself, or returning home. He knew his parents missed him. He missed them as well, and being home, but he knew he'd miss his friends and his life there in California even more. There was no easy answer.

A giggling Laurence came careening into the study room, disrupting his debate and the quiet of the room. The door smacked wide to drift shut at his entrance. Josh took one look at him then grimaced toward Gregory. "What do you think he did this time?"

"Ribbons? Sharks? A pail filled with flour?" Gregory shook his head ruefully. "He's the only one who knows, aside from his victim."

Laurence was panting and grinning from ear to ear when he came to settle at their sides, wiggling to stand between them. In silent agreement, they inched away from him on their seats. Not that it would have done a whole lot of good. Where there was one, usually the other two could also be found. Over the last few months, the three had nearly begun to live in each other's pockets. On and off campus, and more often than not while one was waiting for the others, RJ joined them.

"Who was it this time?" Josh asked him, already feeling sympathy for whomever Laurence had targeted that week. The man had way too much time on his hands with his part-time hours and internship.

"Dr. Nutt."

Both Gregory and Josh groaned. "You better be thankful he's got a great sense of humor."

"And an apathy for revenge," Josh added under his breath.

"Laurence!"

Gregory and Josh winced in unison at the bellowed thunderclap of his name.

"Don't know you," Gregory stated, going back to his laptop. A few seconds later, Dr. Nutt and his fuming anger pounded through the door.

"There you are!"

Laurence tried to look contrite, with wide eyes and batting lashes. Josh knew better than to believe it.

"Laurence Toliver. You are incorrigible!"

"But I'm not boring!" he cried in perfect melodramatic fashion. Then fell to the table in front of him in gasping laughter.

Josh tucked his shoulders inward, trying to look smaller, even though he was sitting right next to where Laurence hugged the table in his hilarity. It took everything Josh had in willpower to not explode in laughter when he glanced up at this week's victim. He gulped air.

"Um, Dr. Nutt. Is that...glitter?" He was coated in iridescent, multi-colored flakes from the top of his arched brow to halfway down his suited chest.

"Yes!" Dr. Nutt barked, then shook out his hands. "My desk drawer. How a student of mine became so proficient at trigger bombs..." He ran his hands down his coat arms, showers of glitter falling loose. "Laurence, you're worse than my own sons, but boy, you need to find another way to use your hours here on campus." He raised and pierced Laurence with a penetrating gaze. The stare in those commanding eyes had Josh sitting straighter alongside him. "Don't lose your internship for stupid pranks."

"Oh," Laurence choked, standing by the table, dumbstruck.

That got his attention. Leave it to one of his victims to finally get through to him. Josh and Gregory both had tried over the last few weeks to convince him to stop the pranks on his old professors. At least Dr. Nutt wasn't vindictive. But Josh was thinking the man did have his limits. And Laurence had already hit him once on his prank spree. The first was a briefcase loaded with expandable snakes that burst like slinkies when he'd opened the case. The shouts had echoed down the hall for almost fifteen minutes while Dr. Nutt had hunted for the troublemaker.

With Laurence gaping like a landed fish, Josh hooked a belt loop in another pair of those skinny jeans and yanked him bodily into his frame. "I'll keep an eye on him, sir. No more pranks."

"Maybe a leash while you're at it," Gregory mumbled, keeping his head and gaze down.

Dr. Nutt gave them all a hard glare then spun. A few paces later, he paused. "Laurence, a word please."

Josh heard him audibly gulp. Laurence walked around the table and approached one of his best loved—while in his class anyway—professors. "Sir?"

Just as Laurence faced him, Dr. Nutt popped his hands out of his coat pockets where he'd settled them after dusting himself off, and repaid the favor. In two fistfuls, he showered Laurence with explosive puffs of glitter.

"Oh!" Laurence cried while ducking and wincing, taken completely by surprise.

"Payback's a bitch, Mr. Toliver. A bitch. Just remember that," Dr. Nutt warned with an evil cackle in his voice and a matching grin. Then chuckling under his breath, he sauntered out of the room, leaving Laurence standing there with his mouth hanging open, a victim of his own making.

When the doors closed behind Dr. Nutt, Gregory and Josh lost it, howling in unison. Laurence shook himself like a dog, making Josh gasp and guffaw louder. The dirty looks he got from Laurence didn't help calm him any, either. With blond hair askew and narrow-eyed glares, he just didn't look mean to Josh. The man was simply too cute to look mean.

That realization made Josh laugh harder.

Stomping to the table, Laurence raked stiff palms down his face. "Ha ha," he barked when he reached Josh, flicking glitter-coated fingers at him. He was far less effective than Dr. Nutt had been.

Josh fought to control his laughter, abrupt snorts escaping between breaths. Gregory was even less successful in stopping his outburst.

When he was closer, Laurence shook himself, spreading the glitter. Instead of being upset, Josh helped clean him off, passing light fingers over trim shoulders and down his arms. "At least it's your color," he remarked with a dry attempt at a straight face.

Gregory almost fell out of his chair, holding his side. Josh pursed his lips, struggling to not laugh further with Laurence right in front of him. Laurence may be small but he packed a wallop of a right hook when he wanted.

"How long did it take you to think up that one?" Josh asked.

Laurence beamed for a short second, proud of his accomplishment. "Not long. Timing was the problem. He locks his door a lot."

"With cause," Gregory interjected, swallowing more guffaws.

Josh studiously removed the specks from around Laurence's neck. "Last one?" was combined with an arched eyebrow.

"Last one," Laurence bemoaned, dejected to have his fun thwarted. He offered one of those bewitching smiles a moment later that always made Josh's skin tight as he tilted his chin, giving Josh room to work. Josh focused on his task to not let Laurence see what touching him was doing to Josh. They'd grown, maybe not closer, but friendlier, since their talk a few weeks before. Josh was struggling with what he suspected.

There were vivid memories of high school, of prom, and Josh was beginning to realize how much of what he'd been doing, how he'd been living, were just the motions, peer expectations. Even sex. It was no wonder, really, that he didn't have a steady girl. He'd thought he'd just been rushing, not having found the perfect match, the woman he would fall in love with. His parents had been high school sweethearts, married for more than twenty years. He'd never suspected that he could be... He didn't let the thought freeze him when it occurred.

Gay.

His school was small, his town was small. He realized if there were gay people in his community, he'd never aligned himself with them, as one of them, because by his family's standards, he couldn't *be* gay.

After four years, and a lot of thinking, especially when Laurence was around, things were becoming clear.

Even when he dated a girl, it was one date, always leaving him feeling empty because something just never connected. He'd blamed it on his class schedule. He was driven to get his degree, distracted. It just had never felt like a priority to continue with any of the girls he knew. Laurence though... He found himself smiling more, relaxed around the other man.

The attraction he'd felt and had fought almost since the beginning wasn't a battle zone for him any longer. He wasn't sure when it became clear, but now he knew what was causing the tingling of anticipation whenever Laurence was nearby. The scariest thing—Josh had no idea how to be gay. Laurence was a man unto himself, wild, bright, unruly, and unafraid. Josh was still cautiously circling the revelations, poking them, waiting for something to either bite back, or explode.

The idea that explosion could be one of glitter made his lips twitch.

"What?" Laurence's fists rested on his hips, piercing eyes watching him like a hawk.

"Nothing," he replied. Total evasion. Josh wasn't ready to share his thoughts on the matter.

Gregory's cell phone rang. Josh was pretty sure the caller was RJ by Gregory's end of things. He listened with half an ear, lifting Laurence's hair to shake out clinging glitter. The strands flowed over his fingers, a pale yellow river of silk. Laurence had his bangs and a little more spiked, while the rest flowed into a shoulder-length pool of pale morning-sunlight blond.

"Sure. Let me ask the other two." Gregory twisted to speak over a shoulder. "RJ wants to get together."

"Where?" Laurence asked, sweeping hands down his arms.

"Club Six? Do you know that one, Laurence?"

Laurence stilled, staring at Gregory unblinking. "Wow, he must be in a mood. Yeah, I know it. Be prepared. It's not for the faint of heart."

Josh spun Laurence, cleaning his back. No one suspected the truth: That he was simply touching because he could, to examine the whys and how it felt later. It felt good, and accepting that as inarguable, he knew he wanted more. Facing the fact no longer strangled Josh until he was unable to even breathe. There was some control to his tentative steps to break down the mystery he'd been handed the day he'd met Laurence.

Josh didn't want Laurence's ridicule if he found out what he was doing, either. He didn't expect Laurence to feel anything for him. Josh hadn't exactly made it easy for him over the years to even be likeable. The fact that Laurence allowed him to be close as he was right then, to touch him, to be near in any way was a vast improvement over the countless arguments they'd shared, usually because Josh had been frustrated and insecure, while holding Laurence responsible for it all. Josh had been less than fair to the man in front of him over the years. He guessed the best he could do now was just be a friend, and hope that Laurence didn't throw it back in Josh's face.

Scooping down Laurence's spine, Josh halted his motions above the waist of Laurence's jeans. *Another* pair of skinny jeans. He hated and loved them. Hated that Laurence wore them for anyone and everyone to admire the way they curved and shaped to his body and loved them because of *exactly* how they accentuated his lithe build. They shaped his ass into two perfect round peaches and gazing at them, he imagined sinking his teeth into them. He shifted on his seat, derailing the hard-on that seemed to happen nearly effortlessly with Laurence around.

"How so?" Josh asked the man in front of him while Gregory finished getting the particulars from RJ. Distractions had to help, right?

"It's um... How to put this for the homophobes in the room."

Josh popped him on that same perfect ass with an admonishing hand. "Quit that."

Laurence twitched then glanced behind him.

"Thought we'd reached an understanding on that, glow stick."

Laurence's eyes twinkled. "And how is that, caveman?" he retorted, twisting to put a hand on a hip to partially face Josh, grinning in challenge. *Just like always.* Only this time, Josh was not going to let it deteriorate into a fight. He would prove once and for all that he accepted, and frightening as it was, even liked Laurence.

The question was how.

CHAPTER FIVE

"I'LL GO WITHOUT a single complaint and I won't say one word about anyone there."

Laurence studied the serious expression on Josh. He almost believed him. Unfortunately, Josh didn't have a great track record when it came to being on Laurence's and RJ's turf. "Not one word? That'll be a miracle."

Josh's scowl, almost an automatic reaction to anything Laurence told him, appeared. Laurence straightened, realizing that Josh's hands had slowed to rest on his hips. They fell away when he spun to face Josh. He would never understand the man. Josh didn't even like him, yet here he was touching him. Josh leaned into his chair, staring up at Laurence with expectant eyes.

"Okay," Josh drawled, crossing his arms, not breaking eye contact. "If this place is that rough, what should I expect? The last time we went to a Laurence club, you forgot to warn us how many of them would be in drag."

Laurence gurgled, then slapped a hand over his mouth to catch the braying laugh. That *had* been a little underhanded, but damn, so much fun! "Not my fault you hit on Timmy."

"Not your fault?" Josh sputtered, his jaw dropping open. A large hand pushed on

Laurence's chest. "You did that shit on purpose."

Of course he did, but he'd never admit it. Torturing Josh was one of his favorite pastimes.

"Timmy did like you," Laurence offered in a conciliatory tone. "He's usually not that...erm...friendly with the customers. They get paid to entertain. They are professionals underneath it all. Apparently you have a thing for willowy blondes."

Josh visibly shuddered at the teasing.

Laurence still remembered what had happened that night, a Christmas party Laurence had tickets for, and the shock on his friend's face afterward when Josh learned the truth. He was sure Josh was going to crucify Laurence for it. Josh had kissed Timmy under the mistletoe. Had more than kissed him. He practically ate "Lavonne's" face. It took two months before Timmy stopped harassing Laurence about Josh, wanting him to bring the big lug back to the club. Timmy swore up and down Josh was gay.

Laurence would definitely go with confused, at least that night.

"It's nothing like that. Club Six is a shark tank, okay?" It was a lot more than that, but he didn't want to frighten them into not going.

"A shark tank?" Even Gregory turned and tuned in at that.

"It's a huge pickup bar. Well, maybe not huge in space, but it's worse than a revolving door with no brakes."

"So RJ wants to get cruised?" Gregory's eyebrows rose.

"Doubt it." Laurence grimaced. "He's not the kind to lay the trap. He must be feeling like shit though, because unless you're an ugly sister, everyone gets hit on there."

"Everyone?"

Laurence swept to Josh, seeing him fade to an eerie shade of green. He leaned close and patted Josh's cheek. "Don't worry, caveman. I'll protect you." Then because Laurence really couldn't *not* be evil, he added, "Just don't wear anything too loose, or washed out. Dark is better." *Especially with your coloring and eyes.* Laurence could picture it and liked it way too much.

"Laurence..."

He shook his head, determinedly giving Gregory an innocent expression. "It'll be fine. Trust me." He would suggest leather, but that would definitely make them suspicious. The thought of Josh in tight jeans was more than enough to make his blood race.

Yum.

JOSH HID HIS hands in his pockets, rounding his shoulders in a little. "Do we have to stand in line?" he whined. He didn't dare look around. The last time he did, egged on by curiosity to see just where Laurence had dragged him, some guy a few behind him blew him a kiss. *The things I do for friends,* he thought, griping under his breath.

Laurence ran a hand over his arm, soothing. "Relax."

If it were anyone but Laurence giving him that suggestion, he might have. Josh had already accepted he'd been duped—again. Club Six was *not* your typical type gay club, or what he could have safely presumed to be a typical type anything club. There was more visible leather, and exposed chests than he wanted to even try to count, all standing with barely restrained impatience to be allowed through the doors where pounding music and the garble of a lot of voices could be heard.

When a few minutes later, a young man stomped off from the front of the line, Laurence pointed out, "That's why we have to do this. They have to check IDs. He probably had a fake one."

"Fine," Josh groused. He hated being on display like this. And it would be the *last time* he took Laurence's suggestion for anything. The snug jeans he wore weren't any worse than anything else he'd covertly noted, other than the men with leather pants, which he just couldn't do, no way. He wore a dark royal blue button down shirt. No, it wasn't a T-shirt, or something more torn than whole, which had been Laurence's choice, but he wouldn't embarrass his friends. He did it to try to fit in, to not stand out too badly and ruin it for either Laurence or RJ. This wasn't his stomping ground, but the other two tagged along regularly with Gregory and himself. He could do this.

He thought he could, anyway.

Josh flinched and tried to scoot forward in the tight line. "Someone pinched my ass," he hissed, bent close to Laurence.

Laurence whirled and glared at the couple behind them. "Hands off. He's here with me and he's not available."

"Oooh, sorry honey," one cooed with a blatantly mocking tone.

Josh twisted and growled. "I'm not—"

"Interested!" Laurence cut him off to tug on his elbow sharply and make him move forward. He jerked Josh close. "Do *not* say you're straight. Not here. Okay?" Anxiety dimmed the usual light in his bright blue eyes.

"O-okay," Josh stuttered. "Why not?"

"It makes you a challenge. They'll stalk you all night long."

Josh stood up. "Oh," he mumbled, getting a clue.

"Aww, how cute. The pretty boy faggot has one on a leash."

Josh snapped straight at the deriding, sneering voice. His first thought was the trio of men had balls to taunt and toss out bullshit to a line of about thirty *more* men waiting to get into Club Six. Especially since he didn't doubt for a minute that the ones in leather four ahead of him in the line could take them one on one and leave two on the sidelines to keep score. They were tall and broad like he was. The four had talked quietly and only briefly paid any attention to anyone else in the line. Two from the four had looked up and nodded congenially to Josh. They were as tall as he was, which made him stand out, but at least tonight, he wasn't alone being the only one who could touch the sky without a footstep.

Josh straightened to his full height and withdrew his hands from his pockets.

"So who's the bitch?" the blond jeered, crossing his arms. For some reason, the three had homed in on Laurence. The heckler's two shadows stood behind him, egging each other on with snickers and tossed elbows. They reminded Josh of high school assholes.

"Apparently, you are," Laurence explained with a dismissive tone. "Your momma's calling." He gave the men his back, facing Josh. His face was stony, but he tried to give a brave smile.

Josh caught the movement in the line and looped a finger in Laurence's jeans, making him follow. For some reason, Laurence lifted a hand and splayed it on Josh's chest. Whether it was to keep his balance or to let Josh know he'd seen, he hadn't a clue. The contact was noticed though.

"So the little cupcake is yours, huh?"

Laurence spun, and Josh could hear his anger building in his chest. Several more in front and behind had begun to pay attention to the pissing contest going on now, too. "You're still here? Go fuck with someone else's life." Laurence gave him the up and down stare. "On second thought, your buddies look ready to plow your ass. You're their bitch. They're drooling for you, honey." Josh couldn't miss the dumbfounded shock and horror on the tweedle-dee twins behind the asshole.

Their antagonist's jaw ground and fists formed at his sides. "What did you say?"

Josh had heard enough. He hooked an arm around Laurence's chest and brought him stumbling flat to his body. He leaned down to growl into Laurence's ear. "Enough! You're going to start a damned street riot." Josh raised his gaze and braced himself. Laurence was *not* going to be someone's punching bag again. "Fuck off, dickheads." He tightened his arm subconsciously. *Mine.* That was when he noted the four that looked like bikers in front of them had also turned and had crossed their arms over their chests.

"If you are finished," one interrupted in a voice that left no doubt he knew how to back it up. In Josh's head, that just made it six to three. Apparently, the trio of assholes could also count. With more dropped slurs they left, flipping off Josh before they were out of sight.

"You better keep a watch on your honey. He's cute and with that mouth," one of the muscular men advised, shaking his head sympathetically.

Josh instinctively snuggled Laurence closer, ignoring the indignant squawk that emerged from him. "We're meeting friends." Who he prayed were already inside.

"Hey, caveman! I'm not a freakin' squeeze toy!"

He loosened his arm, but didn't let him go even when he had to show his ID and pay the cover. Laurence produced his ID from somewhere and they were allowed inside. *Finally.*

Once inside, Josh remembered to close his mouth. He realized immediately that he was overdressed, but it was too late now. A waved arm in the throng caught his attention, and he bulldozed his way through the packed crowd in that direction. A moment or two later he stood before the table where Gregory and RJ sat.

"We saved you some space," RJ shouted over the noise. "Wondered where you were."

"A couple assholes outside tried to start some shit," Josh explained. "The line was long."

"That's short," Laurence corrected him. "It goes around the block usually. We're here early, that's all."

Oh, wow. Josh let Laurence hop onto the last available stool then promptly stood at his shoulder. Drinks were ordered and it was like Laurence had said, within minutes, guys began circling the table, taking in the scenery. And it didn't matter because *all* the guys were looking. He hadn't realized he'd blocked in Laurence until he twisted on his seat and one of his shoulders aligned with Josh's ribs. Laurence gave him an arched look, but neither moved regardless.

"So what's the occasion, RJ?" Josh heard Gregory ask.

"Personal bullshit. I just needed a break. A big break." Black hair danced over his shoulders as he avoided all their worried stares.

"We're here for you, sweetie," Laurence said, no questions asked.

RJ lifted and offered a weak smile. "I know, babe. Thanks. You guys are the best. Even if you are straight assholes." He blinked as he seemed to focus on Josh, as though realizing he was really there. "You too, Josh. I know this isn't your scene."

Josh cupped a shoulder and rocked him lightly. "Friends 'til the end, right?"

"Fuck yeah!" Laurence whooped. "Where's the damn drinks? I want to dance."

Oh, shit! Dance? Josh's legs quaked. He wasn't sure his heart could take Laurence on the dance floor.

CHAPTER SIX

LAURENCE ROLLED a piece of ice over his tongue, smiling with a hint of a tease at a hot stud beneath the strobing lights of the dance floor. Damn, he wanted to touch that tonight. Tight pants, hard thighs, and a round ass to hold on to. The guy's shirt was unbuttoned to his midsection, hanging loose and full of advertising. Laurence's heart beat and he swallowed before he started panting. Dark eyes glittered in the swinging lights when they snagged again in mutual perusal and a slight hike to an eyebrow asked the question.

Ohh, yeah, hot damn!

He stuck an elbow into Josh's middle. "Let me up. I wanna go dance."

"Are you sure?" Josh studied the dance floor, his lips pressed close as he took in the gyrating mob.

"I'll be fine." *Shit, I might even get sucked off if I'm lucky!* He wiggled past a stiff Josh and dashed for the dance floor. The guy he'd been eye-fucking waited for him, a hand held out and Laurence clasped it. He was immediately swept into strong, gentle arms.

"Hello, gorgeous," he purred. "Here alone?"

"With friends," Laurence replied, slinking up along his side to the beat of the music. God, it felt good to let loose again.

"I'm Ted, Teddy if you want."

"Laurence." He raised a hand to a tight shoulder and undulated, groin to hip. "Dance with me good looking."

"It's a start," Teddy replied near his ear, right before licking the skin beneath it.

A shiver sliced down Laurence and he closed his eyes, falling into the magic of the music.

JOSH TOOK OVER Laurence's seat, trying to keep an eye on him in the crowd. It was impossible. RJ slammed down another swallow and thunked his glass down on the table. "It was my mother," he said with no preamble.

"Thought you two didn't get along," Gregory offered.

"We don't, not really." RJ sighed. "Just some hard shit going on right now."

"Because you're gay?" Josh asked.

RJ snorted. "Hardly. She couldn't care less." He flagged one of the waiters. Not a woman in sight. Josh had ceased to be shocked at how little they were wearing. Apparently tips were *very* good on nights like this. With the sea of people and constant motion of fetching and retrieving, there was little doubt the staff ever felt cold, either.

Josh bumped shoulders with RJ. "You got us, man."

"Wouldn't be sane without you guys," RJ admitted. "I really appreciate you guys coming tonight. Don't panic if I disappear for a few minutes."

"Why?" Josh asked.

RJ glanced to Josh, as though weighing something to share. "In all honesty, I'm hoping to get my rocks blown. Once I relax a little, I'll start poking around." He chuckled when Josh's eyes shot wide. "What? Don't you go out to get laid?"

"Well, yeah," he guessed. Not lately, but...

"Same concept. I won't give you the details."

Gregory coughed into his beer. "Thanks for that."

RJ sat up, laughing. "You're quite welcome." He tapped his glass to Gregory's bottle. "Where do you think Laurence went?" RJ mentioned, motioning with his chin to the dance floor. "He's been having eye-sex with a man on the floor for the last half hour."

"Eye-sex?" Josh asked as though trying it out.

RJ started to laugh in earnest. "Oh, man. Virgin ears," he ribbed at Josh. "Dude, we are no different than a man and a woman when we're looking to get lucky. It doesn't take massive effort, fancy dinners or bullshit words when we both want the same thing. You can*not* tell me the whole truth behind easy women *isn't* because they're easy."

"Oh, fuck. So he's out there..." Gregory had set his bottle on the table, sweeping the dancing mass.

"If he's still in the crowd, it's because he's having too much fun dancing. Laurence isn't a pounce and fuck guy. He likes a little build-up. And dancing turns him on."

Turns him on? Oh shit. Josh could understand the need for release. He just wasn't sure how he felt about Laurence being the one *doing* it. Especially with some nameless nobody he'd just met on the dance floor. Fresh drinks arrived and when they'd paid, he tried to find the pale blond hair that he knew so well and swallowed thickly when he couldn't.

"Where would they go?" He leaned close to ask RJ privately.

He raised a hand and pointed. "The restrooms."

"Seriously?" Josh felt ill. The last time he'd found Laurence in a restroom, it had been against his will and being beaten. The memory must have been all over his face.

RJ clutched his arm. "Relax, big guy. Not like then." RJ peered at him hard in the murky shadows of the sidelines where scattered tables were packed with patrons. None of them mattered to Josh. None of them were Laurence. "Why does it bother you? He's not going to get hurt. He might even come back a little less hyper."

"I like Laurence hyper," he said without thinking about it. RJ's dark eyebrows raised like bridges over his eyes.

"Finish your drink," RJ advised, still holding onto his arm. He brought their heads together. "This is our playground. He's going to be okay."

Josh flexed under his fingers, then forced himself to relax. He had a feeling RJ was trying to warn as much as comfort him, but it really wasn't helping. He just wanted Laurence back.

He shied away from actually admitting why it mattered. Why tonight it bothered him so much. Why tonight Laurence finding another person to be with felt like an inflicted wound. Even though he'd told himself earlier he'd find a way to make the man see Josh was here for him, he wasn't sure he was ready to go *that* far. The fact that Laurence was out there, with some nameless stranger bothered him even more than he'd ever imagined. So what did that mean? He sipped on his drink, fighting to see between pressed bodies, or shoulders, or even just to see his blond hair in just a glimpse and failing completely.

A few minutes later, one of the waiters approached and placed a fresh bottle by his elbow.

"I didn't order this," he said, not wanting to receive it by mistake.

The guy smiled and bent close, the scent of a musk cologne and warm skin right under Josh's nose. The man was naked from the waist up, except for an ear piece that was obviously some sort of phone system inside the bar. He glistened with a light sheen beneath the sparking lights. It didn't surprise Josh as much as it may have when he found himself looking twice with him standing next to their table. He looked, but there was something not right. This wasn't Laurence. He focused when the waiter spoke.

"It's from Sean and his group. They're four down to your right. They wanted to say hi." Then the waiter winked and whirled with a swish in his stride to leave Josh with an offered drink and a dazed brain on how to deal with it.

Twisting on the stool, he peered down the tables on his right until he hit a group. One smiled in welcome, motioned for him to join them and Josh's brain froze.

"What do I do?" he blurted to RJ in a panic.

"Why?" Josh explained it, and RJ leaned on his seat to peek around Josh's larger frame. He returned to his position disinterestedly. "Just go tell them thank you and that you're with friends. They're a harmless bunch. I've seen one or two of them here before," he added absently, slurping on his latest order. Something with crème de *something green* in it. Josh would never be a good bartender.

"If Laurence comes back, keep him here," he ordered lowly. He didn't want the other man to vanish again. They needed to have a talk, of some sort, maybe. Sighing and feeling more confused than ever, he palmed the alcohol offering and cut through the crowd to approach the table.

One of the group immediately hopped up and offered a seat when he reached them.

"Thanks for joining us," another said loud enough to be heard over the music, the one who'd smiled. "I'm Sean."

Josh gingerly sat a butt cheek on the stool, bracing himself on a stiff leg. "Josh. Thanks for the drink."

"My pleasure. You're new to Six."

"First time." Josh wasn't sure what to say, but remembered Laurence's warning about mentioning he was straight.

"Your boyfriend? The little blond sweetheart?"

"He's not... We're just friends." Josh bit his cheek to not say more than was necessary.

One of the men crowding around Sean on the bench seat leaned in and petted his chest. Sean kissed his temple. "Thanks, love."

Josh thought they looked like adoring puppies gazing up at Sean the way they were.

"This is Misha, and Natáli. Say hello boys." They both chimed in with gentle hellos, lowered lashes and demure postures showing their deference to Sean. "You seem a little confused," Sean offered with amusement, his lips twitching. Long black hair swept away from Sean's sharp facial features where the man on the left was running fingers through it.

Josh realized he'd been staring. He sipped his beer. Just what kind of club was Club Six after all?

"My boys are mine, make no mistake. I wonder though, if you know where yours is?" Sean arched an eyebrow.

"He's not mine." For the first time, Josh noticed how petulant he sounded.

Sean sat up. "Lingo, take them out to the dance floor. Make sure they keep their clothes on this time."

The man standing chuckled but nodded. Sean gave Misha and Natáli each a quick kiss before shooing them out of their seats. The two men were herded toward the dance floor.

"Come sit by me so I don't have to shout, Josh."

It was a request, but it came from a man who was used to being acknowledged and listened to. Josh figured he had nothing to lose.

"I'm going to explain this, not because I feel the need, but because I believe it will help you." Sean twisted on his seat and rested an elbow on the table. "I love Misha and Natáli. Yes, you heard me right. We are a ménage relationship. It works for us. Lingo is my driver and bodyguard, though in here, he can relax more than at most places. *Here* I don't have to hide. None of us do." Sean paused. "You, my gorgeous god, are hiding."

"Uh..."

Sean raised a hand, a calm smile on his mouth. "I've been watching since you walked in. You're gorgeous, new and unless I've lost leave of my senses, utterly smitten with your golden boy."

Josh stiffened on his seat. "Look, I don't know—"

Sean waved him off. "You can listen, or you can fight it," he continued just as calmly as though Josh hadn't spoken at all. "Both Natáli and Misha are soft spoken young men and either would tear his heart out for me. I love them enough to never want to have to ask it of them. I've seen the way your golden man looks at you, though it is buried and unsure. You, though...you've been searching ever since your man was swallowed onto the dance floor. Maybe keeping him closer will do more for the both of you than pushing him away."

Josh stood from his seat. "Maybe you should mind your own business. We're good friends and have been for years."

Sean shrugged with little care. "Then tell me what a straight man is doing in a gay erotic club. Friendships only go so far."

Josh gulped at the final explanation, but fought to hide it. He was going to kill RJ for this, then maybe Laurence just for leaving him to face this asshole alone. He placed the barely touched beer on the table. "Thank you for the drink. I'm going back now."

Sean gazed beyond Josh's body. "Maybe you should."

Josh spun and he landed on Laurence, who was at that moment, hopping up onto the empty seat.

"Jealous? You can't be jealous over someone that doesn't matter, Josh," Sean whispered, standing at his side. Sean slunk past, a hand on his waist to trail away as he sauntered out to the dance floor to be engulfed by the arms and legs of his two lovers. They kissed passionately between the three of them and no one so much as blinked an eye in their direction.

Fuck me. Two lovers? Josh shook himself. Then what Sean said sank in. He *was* jealous. He was *deeply* jealous of the man Laurence had tripped off to dance with. Of the man he'd probably just had sex with.

He shuddered. *Whoa!* Josh felt like he was about to hyperventilate. How did he feel about Laurence having sex with someone? A fist formed at his side. He hated it. He'd never really thought about whether Laurence had sex. He only occasionally mentioned someone he was dating, as though he was being respectful of not overloading his straight friends with sordid details. Or maybe he just hadn't been that serious about any of them. Josh had no idea. He had never really thought about whether he had sex or not. Laurence was a guy. Of course he did. If Josh did on occasion then there was no reason to expect Laurence to do any less.

Then a stranger approached the table. A hand went around Laurence's back to settle at his waist.

Josh snarled behind clenched teeth. A flash of skin snapped his attention to the dance floor and in unison, Misha and Natáli were both disrobing their shirts, a strong arm around their waists from Sean holding them upright, totally entrusting themselves to his care. Nothing but love and desire shown in any of their faces. Even Lingo held a fond affection as they bumped and ground against each other.

That didn't look so bad. Not the dancing, but the *emotion*. The devotion that was so clear between them. He didn't want to hold Laurence at arm's length any more. Except now that he'd been struck by that epiphany to find out just what this was, Josh wasn't sure he had a chance with the stranger wrapped around Laurence like a climbing ivy.

CHAPTER SEVEN

"HI, GUYS!"

"There you are," RJ grumbled. He looked to his side with a knowing sweep of gray eyes. "Have fun?" Gregory sat opposite waiting as well.

Laurence almost clapped. He felt fucking fab-*u*-lous! Visions of Teddy's mouth... He almost purred, his lashes drooping with the memory of the last ten minutes replaying vividly.

"Never mind. You're smiling too much," Gregory quickly interjected, waving his beer bottle back and forth. "No war stories. Remember the rule. Don't kiss and tell."

Laurence was glad to see they both were still sober. No more floating livers. Laurence laughed loudly. Gregory shook his head in emphasis. "You can't tell me you guys aren't getting any attention. You're hot shit!" Then Teddy arrived with fresh drinks and wrapped a hand to rest on Laurence's jeans waist. "Thanks, hot stuff. Ted. This is RJ and Gregory." He looked around for Josh, but couldn't spot him. Ted shook hands. "Where's Josh?"

"Right behind you," came his deep voice.

"Great! Ted, Josh. These are my friends. We all went to college together."

"Nice to meet all of you." Ted smiled.

Laurence became sandwiched between a standing Josh and a hovering Ted.

"How'd it go with your admirer?" RJ shouted toward Josh. "He's out on the dance floor with those two hotties."

"Fine," Josh said.

Laurence would eat his shirt if he was wrong, but he thought Josh sounded sullen. "Wait. You had an admirer? And I missed it?" Laurence crowed, still flying high on his adrenaline rush. "What did you do? Punch his lights out?"

Josh scowled at Laurence. "No." Something flickered in his eyes, then his dark lashes fell and it was gone. Whatever Josh had been thinking, feeling, about to say sent Laurence's heart into his ribs. What was *that*?

Another man neared the table and tapped RJ on the shoulder. "Want to dance?"

RJ studied the group. "Don't leave me," he mouthed quickly, then stood and followed the hunk in denim to the dance floor.

Laurence was punch drunk, he knew it. He wanted everyone to feel as good as he did right then. Too bad Josh and Gregory were straight. A thumb stroked his spine and he leaned into Ted. Josh wouldn't look at him, his scowl deepening. Laurence worried his face was going to get stuck in that position.

He had thought Josh was getting less sensitive to Laurence, or any of them, and their activities. If he didn't like RJ going to dance or Laurence being close to Ted, well, tough shit.

When someone invited Gregory to dance, he shook his head, his shoulders growing tense. "Sorry. Not tonight." The man at his side offered an open hand in invitation and Gregory gave Laurence pleading eyes.

"He's not into it tonight, sweetie. Maybe another night," Laurence called across the table.

"His loss," he retorted before leaving the table with a ramrod stiff back.

Ted grabbed RJ's vacated stool. "Why don't you feel like dancing?"

Gregory opened his mouth but before he could say anything, Laurence leaned in and gushed, "Josh and Gregory aren't gay. They're here as friends. The best fucking friends on the planet!" he cried, lifting his glass to the center of the table. Gregory tapped his bottle to the drink. Laurence waited and after giving Josh a dark look that accused him of evil things for leaving him hanging, Josh did the same with a fresh beer.

"Really? This isn't freaking you guys out?" Ted sat straight, gaping between the two of them in shock. Now that it was getting late, there was far more bare skin on the dance floor and more men necking and fondling than Laurence was sure either Josh or Gregory had ever been exposed to. It was a massive turn on for Laurence. Live porn! He giggled at his own joke.

"A little," Gregory replied, but with a halfhearted shrug, he showed it didn't matter.

"They're our friends, who would and have walked through fire for us. Being gay is no more important than Laurence being blonde, or Josh being the Jolly Green Giant."

Ted's hand slid to Laurence's thigh. "You are the fucking luckiest son of a bitch on the planet, Laurence. Don't you ever lose these guys."

Gregory winked at Laurence but when he faced Josh, Laurence's heart shot up to his throat. Something hot and secret, and... Oh... Laurence forgot how to breathe when his ribs grew tight around his lungs.

"Josh?" he asked, though it sounded like a husky whimper. A secret door cracked and an electrical current zapped Laurence all the way to his toes. The same door he'd padlocked years ago. One look and there was no holding back the shock of awareness arcing through his system.

"You'll never lose me, glow stick," he drawled, his voice low and undeniably sexy. Before he could figure out *why* he thought that or if he was imagining it, Ted spoke up.

"Glow stick?"

Laurence heard the laughing question, but he couldn't rip himself from Josh's gray eyes. It was almost as though he had to jerk himself free of their pull, and even then he wanted to go back. Wanted to know if he'd imagined it, or if...

Or if what? his brain chided him. *Josh is straight. He can't stand you most of the time.*

Laurence licked his lips. Josh followed the action. A fresh shiver slid down Laurence's arms.

"Uh... Yeah, glow stick," Laurence answered with a shaky breath. "It started our freshman year. He was caveman."

"Caveman I can see." Ted held up a conciliatory hand. "I mean no disrespect, but explain glow stick to me."

Josh sipped on his beer, avoiding looking at him again, as though challenging Laurence to try to answer the question.

Laurence fidgeted on his chair, back and forth. Drawn to look into his face again but fighting it, like a moth to a bright light. And no matter how hard he shoved, that damned door would not close at all. Only this time the voice behind it was whispering things he'd long since put to rest.

He's handsome, and loyal. Look at him. He's at Club Six because RJ asked, because you're here. You want more than friendship and always have. Laurence swallowed, the last whisper sucking the air from his body. That door was officially blown wide open now. He didn't know what had changed, but right then and there, Josh became irresistible. Something he couldn't reconcile burned in Josh's bottomless gray eyes. Laurence barely breathed.

He knew Ted was waiting for an answer, his finger stroking over Laurence's forearm.

"Glow stick was... Uh..." Laurence knew but suddenly it felt like he was sharing something personal and precious, something that was between himself and Josh, and in the recesses of his mind, it always had been. It was theirs.

Josh intervened smoothly, giving Laurence a reprieve. "It started because of his hair. Outside in the sunlight, he always seemed to be glowing."

"I can believe that," Ted murmured close to Laurence, nuzzling him behind his ear. "Your hair is amazing."

Laurence hung on by a tenuous thread to Josh's stare. That wasn't it at all, and they both knew it.

Josh broke away first, that sad, sullen scowl in place once more. The movement of lips on Laurence's neck finally registered and he tipped his head. Ted kissed more in appreciation. Josh didn't look Laurence's way again for a long time.

When RJ returned to the group, he smiled, much more relaxed.

It was the first time ever that Laurence didn't want to stay to shut down a bar. And he definitely didn't want to go home with Teddy.

JOSH DRAINED the last of his drink. He was done. He couldn't take any more of Laurence's making out, or all the hot necking going on around him. Yes, he admitted it. The men pooled around him in various stages of undress doing the same damned thing Laurence was doing was making him hot. He could only guess his defenses had finally been whittled down to something a toy soldier could conquer. He wanted to blame Sean for meddling, but he couldn't. Sean had only made him see through his fear, to stop hiding behind it. Straight or gay, it really didn't matter. He wanted Laurence. Except now, it looked like it was too late to do anything about the slap of revelation. And that made for a very unhappy Josh.

"I'm going home. Anyone want a ride?" He barely looked at Laurence with a hand in his pocket, rolling fingers over his keys. He wanted to run a fist right into Ted's face, so he avoided looking that way as much as possible.

"Wait! You were my ride," Laurence piped up, sitting tall on his stool like he'd been goosed.

"I'll get you home, baby." Ted didn't even come up for air from where he was nibbling on Laurence like an ear of corn.

Josh ground his jaw. *Just bet you will.* He didn't doubt Ted meant his house.

Laurence put a stiff arm on Ted's shoulder. "I appreciate it, honey. I do, but I came with Josh."

"I can take you home," Ted repeated, a confused slackness on his face. Josh guessed he was more drunk than he had been an hour ago. Josh hadn't been paying attention to how much anyone else was sucking down, nursing his own drink. Josh guessed Ted was okay looking, dressed halfway decently. At least he was still wearing everything he'd shown up in.

"I'm sure you can," Laurence placated. He kept that stiff arm up, effectively blocking Ted's advances now. "But I came with a friend, and I'm going to leave with him."

Josh felt a lot better when Gregory and RJ stood as well. He didn't want to be anyone's wet blanket, but he'd hit his limit. Limit of drinking and most definitely his limit of watching and hearing Laurence make those little gasped moans. He was *done*.

Ted huffed, then glared at Josh, blaming him for not getting lucky twice. "Fine. Give me your number."

That sounded way too much like a demand to suit Josh and grabbed Josh's attention, whipping him to scowl toward Ted. Josh shifted to stand right behind Laurence. No one treated Laurence without respect. "Was that an order?"

"What is it to you?" Ted swayed, glaring fully at Josh now. "Give me your damned number, Laurence."

"Uh, no, that's okay. I'll see you around, Ted." Laurence slid from his seat and sidled up under Josh's arm. Josh swept him close without a single complaint. What surprised him was when Laurence came to him without hesitation.

"Damned teasing bitches. You're all the same," he barked. "Damned drama queens and twinks. Is this a game you two play? Is he your bitch?" He snarled at Josh, gesturing rudely to include Laurence. "Fuck! My wife gives better head than you do!" It was an irate scream that at least five other people heard.

Josh's fist was in Ted's face before he knew what he was doing. Ted's arms whirled like propellers and he crashed into a table, sending glasses and guys flying.

Two guys he didn't know gripped Ted around his arms and hauled him from the table where he lay stupefied. He was unceremoniously dragged somewhere and forgotten.

Then Josh realized what he'd just done. *Shitshitshit*. Were they going to call the police? Would Laurence ever talk to him again?

Things began to register slowly. The pounding of the music. The bright flicker and sway of the lights. "We better get out of here." Laurence was tugging on his hand. Gregory and RJ were gaping, but encouraging him to get his ass moving too.

Josh gazed around, looking for more bouncers or whatever. A couple of waiters were cleaning up the table, but other than that and a few curious stares, no one was giving him much attention. The club was just too packed. Small favors.

Laurence clasped his hand in a tight fist and Josh followed his tugs blindly.

"Josh?" Someone shook his shoulders. "Josh?"

He made himself focus. They all stood outside on the sidewalk, now away from the club entrance. "Gregory? Is everyone okay?"

"We're fine. What was that?" Gregory asked.

Laurence was still holding his hand, running a palm up and down his forearm. Josh couldn't believe how good it felt. He never wanted to let him go again.

"I don't know," he replied. "I didn't like how he was talking and—"

Laurence lifted a hand and pressed warm fingers to his lips. "Let's get out of here before they do something about it, okay?"

Josh nodded stiffly. "Right. See you guys later?"

"You bet." Gregory waved and jogged across the street, RJ going with him, but splitting off in another direction.

"Josh? Caveman? C'mon, Let's go."

CHAPTER EIGHT

SOMEHOW, LAURENCE wrangled him into the car and got him to sit behind the wheel, gripping it. "I'm so sorry, Laurence." He could barely whisper it, he felt so awful. When Laurence didn't answer, his heart wilted a little. He didn't dare look at him. Drawing a breath to get through the next twenty minutes, he started the car.

Neither spoke on the drive, and Josh didn't push for it. He'd been an ass. He had no right to deck Ted, no matter how good it had felt. Well, no reason until the end there when he'd admitted to being married. That was low, using guys like that.

"Come up to my place for a few minutes, Josh. Let me look at your hand."

Laurence spoke gently, and Josh agreed, grateful Laurence wasn't screaming and yelling at him. Maybe that was yet to come. Josh didn't know.

He followed Laurence, who'd worn another pair of skin tight black jeans, his cute little butt swaying as he hopped up the stairs that split the house into sections. Josh was transfixed by the sight. Then the key was in the lock and the door was open. Josh felt numb. He'd *never* just laid someone out like that.

"Come on, big guy." Laurence urged lightly and Josh went obediently. "Sit on the couch."

Josh did. A moment later, Laurence returned carrying a small first-aid kit. "You must have nicked a knuckle on his teeth. At least the bleeding stopped."

Josh looked down. He hadn't even noticed, spotting the blood trails on the back of his hand. His mouth was bone dry with Laurence caring for him, touching him. He lifted slowly. Laurence sat on the table directly in front of him, apparently absorbed in what he'd done to his hand. "I'm so sorry, Laurence. I shouldn't have—"

Laurence stopped him again. Warm fingertips. Josh's heart danced at the slightest pressure.

"I wasn't going to give him my number, or go home with him. He was for the night. Fun for then. I'd already told him that twice. It's his own fault for pushing it. Though I had no idea he was married." Laurence let out a dejected breath. "Unless they're perfectly honest, you never know."

Laurence was bent over Josh's hand, carefully examining the scrape and wiping it down with a towelette.

"Was he fun?" Josh hated himself for asking, but he had to know. Was that the type of guy that Laurence liked? Slick and unremarkable? He'd seemed very boring and self-serving to Josh, but then again, he hadn't spoken to the sleaze, wasn't about to, either.

"For a little while," Laurence replied. "What about your admirer?" Swift as a darting sparrow, those blue eyes flicked up then dropped.

Was he curious? Jealous, maybe? Josh hoped so.

"A guy bought me a drink. Gave me some advice. Apparently, it was pretty obvious I am straight." His lips twisted ruefully. He'd thought he'd at least dressed enough to look non-descript. Sean had seen right through him.

Laurence snapped up, his hands light, but his shoulders stiff. "No! Please tell me he didn't say anything or hurt you. I never wanted that."

"Shh," Josh murmured, flexing the hand Laurence was caring for, threading Laurence's smaller one into it. "He didn't tell me anything that I wouldn't have figured out eventually."

Silence sank between them. Something raw and hungry snapped in the air between them with their gazes locked on one another. "Wha-what did he say?" Laurence croaked. His soft pink lips were parted, rough pants slipping from him. He didn't move a muscle.

Josh drew a breath, steadying his nerves, then pulled oh-so-gently on Laurence's clasped hand. "That instead of letting you go, I should have been doing this." He brushed his lips to Laurence's. Crystalline blue eyes shot wide. Josh felt the shocked exhale of Laurence's breath on his own lips.

Josh's heart pounded. Blood heated until he was sure he was going to combust. It was a slow, soft sweep. They didn't close their eyes. The strength of that single touch was more than enough to harden him with a volcanic desire where he sat. He reveled in the new heat, the hunger. He'd stopped fighting it completely. He'd never known anything better.

"Josh?"

Neither moved. Both stared hard into each other.

"Yes?"

"You just kissed me," Laurence rasped.

"I know." Josh squeezed his hand. Color was filling Laurence's cheeks. The beat of his pulse under his skin was obvious, erratic. Josh felt the same way. "Can I do it again?"

Laurence didn't speak. He licked his lower lip then very slowly, nodded.

Josh raised his other hand and tenderly threaded it through Laurence's silken hair. "So pale, so soft," he murmured. "Beautiful." Then he brought them together.

Laurence went supple beneath his hands, bending and twisting for Josh's kiss. Long lashes fluttered and hid those baby blues and Josh did the same, sinking into the newness, the raw heat of something he'd never tasted.

The skidding press of a flat palm floated over Josh's shoulder and he fought to not tense, waiting for Laurence to push him away, to start screaming at him. To call him all the awful things he knew he was due.

What he did made Josh moan instead. Laurence's seeking fingers cupped the back of Josh's neck, light and caressing. Josh drifted his weight back, dragging Laurence up to his feet without releasing his lips or his hand. Laurence didn't fight the silent request, rising to straddle Josh's lap.

The air in Josh's lungs shuddered out in surprise when Laurence settled on him, his light body filling Josh's lap and his vision. He wasn't rail thin, just sculpted, lithe, almost wiry but better. Josh groaned when they separated from the sweetest kiss of his life.

"Josh?" Laurence's voice was shaking, low and confused, but definitely not angry.

"Yes?"

"What happened to being straight?"

Josh caressed Laurence's jaw with a thumb, tracing Laurence's face with fingertips and his gaze. "Honestly, I don't know."

"Are you drunk?"

Josh's lips quirked, just a little. He felt like he was floating, but... "No, not drunk."

"Then... Why?"

"I really don't know. Something snapped tonight. I hated seeing you with Turd."

Laurence smiled, his eyes glimmering knowingly. "Ted."

"Whatever."

They chuckled together. Josh didn't let Laurence go and he grew solemn. "It's taken me a long time to get to this point, Laurence. Years. Years I gave you hell, and for that, I'm sorry."

Laurence leaned forward, touching their foreheads together. "I forgave you a long time ago."

Josh closed his eyes. "Where do we go from here?"

Laurence straightened but didn't take his weight away from his spot on Josh's lap. Josh couldn't stop from dropping a hand and cupping his hip, keeping him there regardless. Josh didn't want to lose the closeness, this *peace* they'd hit on together. It was like the world was anywhere but there. They were cocooned in a quiet place, an island for just the two of them. Josh liked the feeling a lot.

"I really don't know," Laurence answered. "Why are you kissing me? Just because you were jealous of Ted?"

Josh's head fell to the back of the couch. "Yes. No." He huffed a breath. "I didn't even know that's why you went dancing."

"If you had—"

"I would have chained you to a chair," Josh stated with a hint of steel, and a total lack of remorse. "You don't need some faceless hookup."

"Uh, hate to break it to ya, but I've been without for months. I'm not auditioning for monkhood." Laurence released him, but only partially. Josh still held his hand and he wasn't letting that go.

"Honesty, right? That's what you respect?"

"Completely." Laurence frowned at him. Obviously Josh was disturbing what he knew as the Book of Josh.

"I haven't been with anyone since the last date I had with Rachel's girlfriend, and here's a clue. We didn't have sex."

"Wait." His cute brow tightened. "Okay, Rachel knifed the shit out of Gregory's heart more than six months ago. So any double date you had would have been... A year ago?"

"Bingo."

"How long has it been?"

Josh shrugged. He'd pretty much lost conscious count or concern since he began to paddle for shore over Laurence. "I don't know. A year and a half? Maybe longer."

Laurence's jaw fell open. "But why?"

He sighed. Time for that honesty pill again. And no matter the reaction, he more than owed Laurence this. "Because not one woman turned me on the way a blond and blue-eyed firecracker with a sass mouth drove me insane. I just didn't realize until very recently that it was attraction that I'd been fighting."

"Me?" Laurence squeaked.

"Yes, you."

Laurence rose from Josh's lap. Realizing Laurence had probably just been served a full plate of Oh-My-Fucking-God, Josh let him go, albeit reluctantly.

The longer Laurence stayed silent, the more Josh worried. He wasn't pacing or mumbling, just standing there in the middle of the living room, the trash from Josh's little medical emergency on the table forgotten. Laurence's apartment wasn't large enough to allow for a lot of angst-filled pacing to begin with, but still. Josh felt a chill overtake him when silence reigned.

"Laurence?"

He shook his head in answer and Josh's shoulders sank inward, his hands finding his pockets when he stood from the couch.

"I'm sorry. I guess I should've just left well enough alone." He walked around the table but stopped at Laurence's shoulder. "We are still friends. I meant what I said. You won't lose me."

When Laurence remained in place frozen, Josh accepted his mistake, even though it felt like it was honestly breaking his heart to be so wrong. He circled around him for the door.

"Wait."

Laurence's near silent plea froze him solid to the floor.

"So now you're gay? Suddenly gay?"

He raised a shoulder. "I don't know what I am, Laurence. Not sure I really care or that it even matters. I do know I care about you. I know it killed me a little once I knew why you'd disappeared, though as RJ pointed out, I am definitely a gay virgin." He tilted his head on his neck. "I was worried about you, Laurence. I don't want to see you hurt again."

Realizing he was probably rambling pointlessly, he opened the door and let himself out after a faint goodnight. He couldn't stand there and continue to see Laurence's confusion and not read it for what it was—rejection. How could he expect anything else when he'd been tormenting Laurence for years?

Once home, he walked to his bedroom and stripped, taking a very hot shower to erase any stink of the night off his skin. The only memory he wanted was of Laurence and his kiss, and that wasn't hard to fulfill.

He'd been falling asleep with the man on his mind for months now.

This was just the first night he'd ever gone to bed with a hard-on for him and accepted unequivocally Laurence was the sole cause behind it. He couldn't curse him for it. There was no one to blame but himself for the hollow pain he felt. If he'd been a little less asinine... If he'd been a little more willing to bend, to see what was happening... Maybe things would have gone a little better when Josh admitted how he felt. Instead, it had taken most of four years and a lot of ignorant crap with Laurence taking the brunt of it. His mistake tonight could have also ruined a very good friendship, though he hoped not.

He punched his pillow and stared at the wall, watching the nighttime lights out in the world play through the blinds.

CHAPTER NINE

LAURENCE PAUSED in the apartment building's hallway and knocked. It was brightly lit. He hoped if anyone saw him, he didn't look half as bad as he felt at that moment. He couldn't sleep a wink after Josh left. A necessary change into a clean shirt and shorts along with a quick shower and he still hadn't managed to push the lug out of his head. He tried to be loud enough to wake Josh if he were asleep, but not anyone else. It was after four in the morning. All he needed was someone calling the cops on him.

He knocked again, holding his breath. If he couldn't wake him up then he'd go home. It was where he should be. Only...Josh wasn't there. And suddenly that made sleep impossible.

The click of the lock took him by surprise. He'd already prepared himself to accept this foray as a futile effort.

The door swung open. "Laurence?" Josh didn't sound like he'd been asleep. He looked tired, his eyes weary and a little bloodshot. It didn't matter because he'd never looked better to Laurence.

"Can I come in?"

Josh stepped out of the doorway and Laurence entered the apartment. It was larger than Laurence's though furnished about the same, from Garage Sales R Us. The apartment was dim without any lights on. He stuffed his keys in his pocket while Josh shut and locked the door.

"What's wrong?"

Laurence gazed up at the mountain before him. His hair was in disarray, proof he'd either dragged him from bed, or he'd been running his hands through it repeatedly.

"Did I wake you?" He cleared his throat when his voice wavered.

"Wasn't asleep."

Laurence dropped his gaze, feeling himself want to fidget beneath that intense stare. Just like earlier at the club. Something potent in those eyes set off Laurence, and not in a bad way.

Josh was bare from the waist up. He only wore a pair of loose sweat pants, but whether he'd needed them or been wearing them, Laurence didn't know. He had no idea how the man slept, or in what. He couldn't explain it, but suddenly, badly, Laurence wanted to get close to all that skin. Wanted to caress the hard expanse of his chest, the darker skin of his nipples. Wanted to taste them and run his nose through the hair between his pecs.

"Laurence." Josh sighed with a touch of impatience. "It's late. Why are you here?"

"Why did you kiss me?" he asked, trying to make it a demand and failing miserably.

"I told you why."

Laurence trembled. "If... If I asked, would you do it again?"

"Don't do this, Laurence. I'm sorry, okay?" Josh carded a stiff hand into dark, disheveled hair and swept it away from his features. "We're still friends. Best friends."

Laurence growled out his name, his hands forming fists as his patience grew thin. He wasn't sure how much longer he could hold it together, wasn't sure what it was he was searching for. And definitely had no idea why he couldn't stop this. He only knew he hadn't imagined what he'd felt earlier between them already, but Josh had left before he'd come out of the shock of being kissed by one of his closest friends.

A long breath raised Josh's shoulders as indecision warred with something Laurence knew he should recognize on his face. Josh battled in silence. They stared at each other, neither budging, both breathing a little harder. Then something in Josh's gaze lit, burned, and heat poured off Josh's torso in front of him. Gentle palms cupped Laurence's face and raised him, held him and he couldn't look away. Steel gray eyes pierced him, held him immobile. "Are you sure, Laurence?"

He quaked all over. "Yes." He could barely breathe, but for this, he was sure.

Josh bent and hovered over his lips, hesitated a hairsbreadth away. After a long heartbeat, Laurence raised on his toes and closed the gap.

Laurence had never been kissed like his was the last kiss anyone would ever know. Like his kiss was a gift. His throat worked hard and thinking became difficult. Because the slow, simmering passion held in check behind Josh's kiss was all of that and so much more. Soft and gentle, Josh danced his lips side to side, shooting tingles and awareness deep to Laurence's core, a place that until that moment, had never been touched. Blood rushed through his body, a heat wave that slammed into his groin with need.

He lifted his arms and encircled Josh's neck, their height difference causing him to bow naturally into Josh's frame. The shock of contact was bone deep and electric. He whimpered and clung, craving more touch, more heat, more of Josh, as close as they could possibly get.

Josh's hands caressed, flowed and eventually settled at Laurence's waist. The sweep of his thumbs finding their way beneath his shirt to stroke skin sent butterflies into Laurence's belly. They were both panting heavily when Josh broke their kiss.

"Is that what you wanted, Laurence?" he asked, hoarse, trying to catch his breath, his eyes wide and bottomless and searching.

Laurence gulped, trying to get words from his brain to his mouth, and failing.

Josh's fingers tightened at his waist. "Why are you here?"

Laurence wished he knew. Nothing had made sense since Josh's first kiss a couple hours before. Josh slowly stood, though he didn't release where he held Laurence in his hands.

"I don't know!" Laurence wailed. He bit his lip. "This isn't making sense. You—"

Josh pressed his lips to Laurence's and he shut up on a sputter. He felt his legs weaken under the passionate assault and tightened his hold on Josh.

The hands that held him slipped around his body and cupped his ass in firm grips. In a fluid motion, Josh plucked him off the floor and Laurence automatically hooked his legs around Josh's waist. Laurence shuddered with a deep moan bubbling in his throat. Secured tight against Josh's body with his hands spread over his back to hold him there, he barely noticed when Josh began walking.

Laurence wasn't thinking. He couldn't. Josh teased him with the tip of his tongue, flicking but not giving him what he wanted. Instead, he circled Laurence's lips, painting them over and over until Laurence was a mass of nerves about to scream in frustration to deepen their kiss.

Cool sheets on his skin brought him a little out of the fog. They were in Josh's room, on his bed. And Josh was gazing down at him like Laurence was his entire world. His heart tripped several times.

"Josh?" Laurence whispered. He slid fingers into Josh's hair, discovering the richness on his skin. He'd always wondered and couldn't help himself now.

"Shh," he replied. He pulled up the blankets and covered them both. A few more kisses, gentle and light and Josh sighed. "Goodnight, Laurence." An arm snaked beneath Laurence's shoulders and the other rested with a hand on his hip as they faced each other.

"Goodnight?"

"Sleep for now," Josh explained. "This is good." He opened his eyes and locked with Laurence's. Deep black lashes circled cloud gray eyes. Not just gray, but spring storm gray. And so warm and caring. When was the last time someone had looked at *him* like that? "This is perfect. Always has been. Give me a chance to catch up. Please?"

Laurence lay there, in his arms, stunned. Finally, he nodded and the sheer joy in Josh's expression stole Laurence's ability to deny him. Josh was truly happy, and Laurence was the reason.

He was scared to close his eyes. He knew when he woke up, it would prove to have been a dream. Laurence knew this wasn't real. How could it be? But held in strong arms, while the heat of their bodies washed over him, he fell asleep dreaming about those kisses and wanting more of them. From Josh.

JOSH SIGHED, a deep rumble that was nothing but pure contentment. Lips were casually drifting beneath his jaw. Teeth scraped the rough of his stubble over his Adam's apple making his toes curl.

Wait. *Lips? Teeth?* He popped completely awake and lurched backward. He blinked dazedly at the crooked grin on Laurence's face. The longer he stared trying to make his morning make sense, the more hesitant Laurence became, the more he withdrew and the more that sweet grin wobbled, until finally the mildest spark of pleasure on Laurence's face faded and died away.

"I was afraid this was going to be a mistake," he murmured, staying where he was, where Josh had left him in his abrupt confusion. It felt like a chasm separated them, when it was no more than a few inches.

Josh shook his head, about the only movement he could muster as he tried to bring his world back to rights. Laurence was in his bed. Had been kissing him.

And at that moment was rolling away to climb out of bed.

"No!" He reached blindly and fisted the shirt Laurence still wore, then jerked him with an *oomph* to the bed. He swooped in and covered Laurence's smaller frame. Josh's heart was racing. Christ, didn't the man own any *normal* clothes? The T-shirt was paper thin and he couldn't look at the shorts. He shook himself, trying to focus to keep Laurence there. "Not a mistake." He stared down into beautiful blue eyes, and wished he knew what to say.

"You're addled in the brain, Daily." Laurence thumped Josh on the temple with a finger. "You are not gay. You were drunk last night. You can't stand me. I have lost count of all the—*mmph.*"

Josh shut him up by kissing him. Made sense to him and it was effective. It took about four seconds before a shocked Laurence yanked on his hair and smacked a shoulder with a fist. Seeing defeat, Josh let him go. He rolled completely away, staring up at the ceiling.

"I'm sorry, Laurence. I'm doing this all wrong."

"What is with you?" he snapped.

"Why did you come here last night?" Josh volleyed right back with a slanted eyebrow.

Laurence deflated. "I don't know," he replied weakly.

"There you go," Josh returned. Josh would pay anything for a clue at this point on know how to deal with the dynamite currently in his bed. "I don't know how to do this."

Laurence rocked his head on the bed to stare his way. "Do what?"

Josh shrugged. How do you court a guy? How do you convince the man you care for that you care for him at all when you're not even gay?

And that was the crux. He couldn't say that any longer. Josh cared for Laurence, and had for months. The problem was how could he make Laurence see it? And how could he convince Laurence that he meant it?

"Thought you were going to give me a chance?" Josh muttered a little cross. He threaded his fingers together and settled his hands over his stomach. It was either that or keep touching and exploring, and he doubted Laurence was ready for that yet.

"A chance at what?" Laurence rolled to brace himself on a stiff shoulder, looking at Josh.

Josh didn't move. "Do you remember any of last night?"

"I don't know. You kissed me. That's not normal. Did I imagine it?"

"No. I kissed you a few times." He peeked out of the corner of his eye. "I thought you liked it. I know I did."

"Josh, you were—"

"I was not drunk. Not when you sat on my lap and not when you knocked on my door."

"But to be suddenly gay?" Laurence's voice was coated in pure disbelief. "Proof!" he cried as though he'd found the explanation to the universe's highest equation. He raised to prop himself on an elbow above Josh now, shaking a finger at him. "You hated being at Club Six last night."

Josh made a buzzer sound. "Wrong. I hated watching Turd slurp all over you. I know what you did with him and I hated *that*." He would have given anything to have kept it from happening. He didn't want Laurence touching anyone else, *needing* anyone else. He carefully let out a breath. One thing at a time. The way this was going, he had a long road to walk. Laurence was having as hard a time as he had just getting to there.

"Why? You gonna suck me off?" Laurence challenged, blatant one-upmanship and the score: His point.

Josh swallowed. Caught in his own trap, he couldn't answer. His mouth popped open but no sound came out.

Laurence almost gloated. "Uh huh. See? I'm right. You're not gay."

"Jesus Christ! Give me time!" Josh growled. "Until last night, I'd never kissed a guy, and Timmy doesn't count. I *thought* he was a woman. Now you want me to just hop on board and suck your cock?" He loosened his grip, which had begun to leave marks on his own skin in his frustration. He was shocked at himself that he hadn't stumbled over that. "Laurence, I hated it because I didn't want him touching you."

Laurence's eyes shot wide then dropped to where he doodled with a finger, drawing aimlessly on the sheet at Josh's side. Josh tried to decipher what was twisting through Laurence's thoughts with little success. He'd have better luck separating grains of sand.

He tried one more time. "Why are you here, Laurence?" He adjusted to face Laurence better, his hand caging Laurence's roving one lightly. He almost completely covered him, Laurence's long fingers curling reflexively into Josh's palm. Blue eyes as pale as the morning sky searched for him through long lashes. Josh shuddered as heat swamped him from his chest downward. *Too damned pretty, but is that the right thing to tell him?* He wished like hell he knew.

CHAPTER TEN

LAURENCE STARED at his caged hand. Tingles and little bursting shocks popped where they touched, firing up his arm and traveling down his spine. He'd never expected the attraction he'd kept locked away to come close to being real, something tangible between them. And he'd definitely never expected it to feel this strong now that he'd dared to let the beast poke its head out to check the possibilities. He wanted to throw himself at Josh and cling like flypaper to every part of the man in front of him. Years of pushing it away, of accepting Josh was just not going to happen, was confounding Laurence's view of this new Josh. The one who'd suddenly appeared in the last twenty-four hours.

The one who looked at Laurence like he would scale mountains for him.

The same man who'd decked Ted for being an ass. The same man who held him while they slept like it was the most natural thing in the world.

"So you're gay?" Laurence asked, subdued.

Josh rolled a shoulder. "I have no idea, Laurence." Skin burned beneath the thumb of the hand still holding his. Gentle sweeps that reminded Laurence of their first kisses. "If you need to have it defined, then..." A crease appeared between his eyes as he frowned, taking his answer very seriously. "I think I am," he whispered, his voice low and husky. "Does it really matter?"

Yes it mattered! But shit. Josh kissed him! His brain just couldn't get past that one little fact. He focused on the heat of their skin connecting. *This is Josh.* But it couldn't be. But it was...

But *Josh isn't gay!* He'd said so himself so many times. What changed in the last twenty-four hours? Laurence shivered, stiffening his shoulders because he feared being overwhelmed by it all.

"So you don't hate me?" Laurence couldn't look up. His entire understanding was being rocked. Things that until the day before had been irrefutable. Josh was straight. Gregory was straight. RJ was gay. He was gay. That was the way it had been since...well, since forever. Four guys who'd become the best of friends through the years.

A gentle crooked finger tipped Laurence up. "Laurence, I've never hated you." He shook his head when Laurence scowled. "Hear me out, okay? I have never hated you. I didn't understand you, and from the first day I met you, I felt something, but if I was straight, it couldn't be attraction for you, right? It confused me. You confused me, to be honest." Josh hesitated and Laurence encouraged him to go on. "And except for two little problems with all of this, nothing would have changed between you and me other than maybe my acceptance for who you are because regardless of everything else, we are friends."

Leaning on his shoulder, Josh's loose hand rose and when Laurence didn't balk, he threaded it into Laurence's hair, separating the strands between caring fingers.

"Okay," Laurence encouraged on a shaky note. "What two things?"

"First, I stopped noticing women completely. Sure, they were pretty, but without knowing I was doing it, I was judging every one of them by you. To your beautiful eyes, this insanely soft hair, even your crazy humor and practical jokes. No one makes me laugh like you do."

"And the second?" Laurence couldn't stop himself from asking. Josh's sweetness was melting him into a gooey puddle on the bed.

"The night you were attacked at the bar."

Josh's eyes dropped away, watching the stroke of his fingers along Laurence's temple. Laurence didn't like him hiding. He liked being able to see Josh's thoughts in his eyes.

"I'd never felt that way in my life. It confused me, and that compounded the idea that I hated you, that I was mad at you, blaming you, for some reason. For just an instant, I wanted to hurt them. Badly. For you." He swept a searching, questioning gaze up once then immediately returned to focus with single-minded attention to what his hand was doing. "I also wanted to protect you. It killed me to see you hurt. Last night..." He swallowed and sucked a slow, ragged breath. "Last night, if it would have kept you from needing some nameless hookup, if..."

Laurence heard Josh's throat clog up. His lips pinched into a thin line until they were nearly white.

With a gusted groan, Josh flopped to his back, an arm covering his eyes. "Still doing this wrong," he growled. He smacked the bed with his fist.

"Ted really bothered you last night?" he all but whispered.

"Laurence, it was a miracle I didn't punch him *before* he opened his lying mouth," he retorted without missing a beat. "I wanted to break every finger he touched you with."

"Oh," Laurence murmured, blinking.

So Josh *did* like him, had been insanely jealous of Ted, and was still stretched out in bed half dressed as though there was nothing unusual to waking together in it. Laurence wasn't convinced this wasn't a mistake, regardless. Or that Josh would come to his senses, make some fruit joke and things would return to normal. *Their* kind of normal.

Boring holes into the mattress beneath him, he said, "I came over last night because I needed to know if I'd imagined it." If Josh could rip open his soul, Laurence could give a little.

"Which?" he replied with mild, derisive enthusiasm. "My insanity or my regret?"

"Neither." He was still trying to unravel what exactly the *it* had been. Josh had certainly unsettled his view of everything he knew to be true between them.

Laurence's hand rose to float over Josh's abdomen and with his face covered by a well muscled arm, Josh had no idea he hung suspended over him, midair. So far, Josh had been reaching, connecting. Was it Josh's way of saying more than he could with words? Would Josh understand the same message? Slowly, light as a feather, he let his hand sink flat to the hard wall of his stomach.

A ripple was born, echoed by a sigh of longing.

"You're touching me. Be careful," Josh intoned dryly. "You might get gay germs."

Laurence winced, knowing perfectly well where and from whom he'd heard those exact same words. He searched his calm face, but his arm hadn't moved away from where it rested. Josh wasn't moving at all.

Neither was Laurence.

"So? Maybe I like your gay germs."

A rough chuckle bounced Josh's body at his bratty comment. Warmth infiltrated Laurence's palm. Sensations of smooth skin, the slight tickle of hair that wound above and below his navel, movement as he breathed though Josh made no effort to make him remove his palm. Stretching his fingers, Laurence could reach from the waist of Josh's sweats to the bottom of his ribs.

"Feels good." Josh sighed, letting Laurence do whatever he wanted.

Laurence also noticed how Josh was being affected by his touch. Warmer skin, deeper breathing and a definite growth south of his fingertips. "I'm doing that?" he said with a note of awed amazement.

"You don't want to know how many times that has happened over the last few months," Josh replied with a quirk of his lips. "Especially when you wear those damn skinny jeans." A shiver rolled down Josh's frame. "Worst kind of evil torture."

This was news for Laurence, especially since a lot of his regular wardrobe was "skinny" clothes. "You must have been walking around uncomfortable a lot," he remarked, allowing the hint of a tease to wind through it.

"I was." Josh groaned in mock agony. "Believe me, I was." Josh's free hand on the bed relaxed and flattened but he did nothing else. "Why do you think I rarely saw you during the day? I couldn't do any of my student teaching hours or lessons with a noticeable hard-on. Do you know how many girls, and even a few guys, would have taken it as an invitation?" He scoffed. "Shit. It was bad enough playing dumb to the girls who thought being just a little older than them was a free pass to better grades because I was a student instructor. Grades by proxy."

"Well, you are kinda hot," Laurence offered with a teasing nuance and a twitch of his lips.

"Just kinda? Damn." Josh pouted. "Guess I'll have to start working out again."

That earned Josh an admonishing slap of Laurence's palm. "Okay, fine. You're hot." Laurence began to draw looping circles with a finger over Josh's body where he'd just rebuked him. He sought Josh through lowered lashes. "You were last night."

Josh's arm hitched up an inch or two, bearing an eyeball that instantly became pinned on Laurence.

"I was? You noticed?"

Laurence felt his cheeks burn. "Always do," he replied, not looking directly into those intent gray eyes.

Laurence's eyes fluttered closed when Josh threaded his fingers into the hair at his temple again. He leaned into the light caress of fingers on his scalp. Josh's hands were big and strong, and so unbelievably gentle, he could feel himself wanting to go limp at the attention.

"Give me a chance, Laurence. All I ask is no more guys like last night."

Laurence lowered to rest more on the bed, closer to Josh. "So, you and me?"

A deep though shaky rise and fall of Josh's chest preceded his answer. "Yes."

Laurence bit on his bottom lip, aware his decision could destroy a long-term friendship. Or maybe, just maybe, have that fairy tale ending. He didn't believe in the second, and feared the first like the plague. He didn't want to—couldn't—lose Josh. Losing any of them would be like tearing off an arm. He just wouldn't live through it.

Josh's hopefulness faded as horror darkened his eyes the longer Laurence stayed silent, considering the outcomes.

"Oh hell. You aren't attracted to me, are you? I just ruined everything, didn't I?"

The quivering fear in Josh's voice galvanized Laurence into action. He pounced. Maybe not as cleanly as he would have liked, but in less than a blink he went from lying on his side next to Josh, to mostly covering Josh's body with his own. He wiggled and Josh gulped. Centered, he braced himself over Josh's slightly surprised face looking straight down at him.

"Shut up and kiss me," Laurence ordered succinctly.

A full body shiver started at Josh's shoulders and rolled south. Both hands curled around him and filled with hair, holding him still, cautiously bringing him near, never once breaking the thread of their locked gazes. Laurence's breath snagged, literally hitched at the intensity burning in Josh's eyes. Dark gray thunderheads tumbling with power, lightning that could strike at any time. As though static electricity filled the room, the hair on Laurence's arms stood on end. Josh brought him closer in slow motion, and Laurence was sure his heart was going to burst out of his chest in anxious anticipation. Then their mouths fused together, a melding of skin and heat.

Nervous tension radiated from Josh, feeding into Laurence, making the kiss stiff and awkward. Nothing like what he'd hoped for, but exactly what he'd expected. He knew this was all wrong. Whatever was driving Josh, he was confused and not into guys. Laurence had known it all along.

Disappointed, he almost stopped Josh completely when he realized he knew what the problem was. Josh needed to know that Laurence wanted him. Josh needed to know that his friend was with him on this. One thing Laurence could show him unequivocally: Josh was not wrong about how much Laurence wanted him too.

Realizing he was just as unyielding as Josh, he forced his muscles to go pliant, to mold to the hard planes of Josh's length and almost instantly, Josh did the same. Then Josh became his center, the only person in his world. The perfect heat of their kiss made him burn.

Not a mistake.

The thought, when it happened, was filled with surprise and maybe even a little awe that only lasted a split second before hunger for Josh's kiss swamped him.

Laurence clutched fistfuls of hair, undulating to get the best angle to taste his lips. Then Josh melted him through. He invaded, thrusting into his mouth to do what Laurence had hungered for the night before. He moaned when Josh greedily kissed him, holding nothing back as he learned the contours of Laurence's mouth. Trembles bounced between them and when he shifted his weight, there was no denying the hardness beneath Laurence's hips. Gay or straight, that couldn't be faked.

"Oh...mm," he gasped, riding against the thick cock between them. "Josh." Laurence knew he was whimpering and he didn't care. That hard ridge felt *sooo* good.

Josh's hands roamed and stroked without pause through his hair, down Laurence's spine to tentatively cup his ass.

Laurence gasped and groaned, engulfed by Josh's desires, and realizing he was very happy there. Before the oxymoron of it being Josh causing his pleasure could take root, Josh's hips unsteadily rolled upward into his body as though testing his welcome and Laurence bucked wildly in answer.

CHAPTER ELEVEN

"FEELS SO DIFFERENT," Josh murmured on a harsh gasp into Laurence's mouth.

"Bad?" Laurence sucked air to talk. Josh had kissed all the oxygen right out of him.

Josh paused the ravaging of his mouth, staring at him breathing heavily, his fingers light and caressing, mapping the contours of Laurence's frame where he straddled over Josh's wider hips. "No, not bad," he finally replied. "Feels good."

Laurence hefted himself up and holding steady on a palm, laced questing fingertips through the mat of hair on Josh's flushed chest for the first time. "This is amazing."

"You don't mind it?" Josh's eyes popped wide with surprise.

"No, I love it. Why?"

A blooming heat created rosy apple-blush rounds on Josh's cheeks. "Lori, Rachel's friend, hated it. It's why we never had sex twice."

"Hated it?" Laurence gaped at him. "But you're incredible! This is thick and..." He lowered and finally got to run his nose through the curls. "Oh, *mmm*." He moaned. The scrape and cushion against his skin, the scent of Josh on his senses—it drove him insane. *Color me happy.* He knew he would love it.

A fierce shiver rocked Josh beneath Laurence. "Do that again," he pleaded. Tight fingers clenched his ass in response to Laurence's playful nose-diving of Josh's chest.

"Like this?" he purred, burrowing with hungry lips through the rich, black curls. "Or this?" He hummed against Josh's sternum.

Josh growled, a sound so deep and sensual, goose bumps flared up Laurence's arms.

Laurence panted, resting in the crook of Josh's neck. "Fuck, Josh. You're going to make me lose it." He'd never heard that sound in his entire life.

"I—I haven't even touched you," he rasped.

Laurence wasn't so sure it was even needed as hot as Josh was getting him. A stuttered sigh morphed into a moan when seeking hands slipped beneath Laurence's shirt, splaying over his back.

Pressed together as close as they could get with their clothes still on, Josh twisted to nuzzle at Laurence's throat. The abrasive scratch of Josh's morning shadow stiffened Laurence from his shoulders down. The flicked whip of his tongue on the heels of his touches shot stars over closed eyelids.

"Is this okay?" Josh whispered.

Laurence had to find the strength to murmur his approval. He was melting into overload, lost at sea beneath the encompassing assault to his senses. Josh's hands stroked to reach and tease the curve of his ass with flicked fingertips beneath the waist of his shorts. Testing and returning for more. It was driving Laurence insane.

Josh sucked lightly on Laurence's arched neck in tandem, shooting chills over his skin and down his spine. Laurence began to rock in needy surrender. Staying still and silent wasn't an option.

"Feels so good," Laurence managed. "Don't stop." His lip quivered on an exhale.

Josh's shaft throbbed beneath his hips and Laurence ground down on captured flesh, driving friction in bursts of pleasure up his spine. The pressure was already building. Skin tightened. An orgasm snuck up on him. It wouldn't be denied now after teasing at the promise of release while enjoying Josh's touch.

"Laurence." Josh groaned. The suckle of his lips grew intense. The bite and pull caused Laurence to tremble with explosive desire, firing heat deep into his body. Moans and hot breath whipped over sensitive skin where Josh's ravenous mouth claimed him.

Laurence clung to his broad shoulders like he was a lifeline when Josh's body rocked against his, surging and rolling with powerful thrusts under him. Laurence rode his hips. Josh slid a hand beneath the elastic of Laurence's shorts and covered skin, holding him tight, pinning him groin to groin as they bumped and ground together. Those deep rumbles vibrated through ribs into Laurence's chest, kicking Laurence's heart into a new gear. If he got the rest of his life to hear that sound, he'd never get enough of it.

"Laurence, please," Josh growled. "So good."

Gliding chest to chest, hip to hip, his balls grew tight. The slightest tease of a finger on his crease, testing. Then Josh was kissing him, striving upward and rocking into him with forceful pumps of his body. Laurence rose and fell with him, dying in little shocks as his body wound tighter and tighter.

Teeth snagged and nipped at flesh on his neck capturing a group of nerves right beneath the skin, catapulting the burning need for release into his blood. Laurence arched, crying out as his orgasm struck like a tidal wave, long and powerful, pulse after pulse, sucking the strength out of his body in pure bliss.

JOSH PANTED, shaken and shaking. Shocks struck when Laurence twitched, dragging whimpered moans from a raw throat. He couldn't move, instead clutching Laurence as close as he dared beneath his palms. Slowly, he relaxed, the weight of his head sinking deep into the pillow as muscles slackened in the aftermath of the strongest release in memory. His dick twitched as his heart recovered. Laurence followed him, resting on a shoulder, puffs of breath drifting to overheated skin.

The gentle pet of a light touch stroked his hair a few moments later. "You still in there, caveman?"

He swallowed, searching for his voice and moisture. "I think so." He couldn't open his eyes. Uncertainty of what he'd actually find made his lids as heavy as anvils.

"Are you all right?" Laurence's worry was plain in his voice. The petting never slowed.

"I'm coming to terms," Josh explained.

"With?" Laurence lowered to whisper into his ear. "Talk to me. In case you weren't here for the last few minutes, we both did that."

That did it. He popped his eyes open. Remembering where his hands were, he tugged the one out of Laurence's shorts and smoothed his T-shirt down again with the other. Seeing disappointment and hurt beginning to dim the glitter that was Laurence's gaze, he formed his hands to his jaw, holding him still. "Don't move. Don't leave," he corrected.

"So which is it? Moving or leaving that I can't do?"

Josh rolled his eyes. The man would never change. Some part of him was glad to know it. "Don't leave, though you don't have to move unless you want to."

Laurence settled himself on a bent elbow cradling his head in a palm, able to gaze down at Josh. "I'm good."

Unsure if it was too soon to make the typical reply to that phrase, he left it untouched by the usual sarcastic banter. Their paradigm had shifted and Josh wasn't sure how safe the footing was for him, for them. Laurence didn't poke, didn't prod, or push. Just remained in contact, touching and petting and letting Josh absorb it all.

He gazed up into patient blue eyes when he felt he'd finally be able to speak and make more than just animal grunts. "Are you okay?"

Laurence grinned with cheeky impertinence. "Fabulous, though a shower wouldn't hurt."

Aware of the sticky, oozy feeling within his own clothes, he grimaced. "I can't remember the last time that happened."

Laurence gave him a playful, shocked expression. "An orgasm?"

Josh tugged lightly on a swaying hank of hair. "No, shot in my pants."

"Bet we could do it again." Laurence neared from where he lingered, blanketing Josh's body with his own, his lips right over Josh's. "But think how much more fun it would be *without* clothing," he purred.

Josh shivered. *Naked? With Laurence?*

"Relax, caveman. I'm not going to molest you."

Searching for and landing on Laurence's amused stare, Josh huffed a breath. "I know, it just feels...weird," he lamely finished.

"Is it the voice or the lack of boobs?"

Josh rumbled a calmer chuckle. "Neither. You're fine." Josh stroked a finger down Laurence's throat to his shoulder. He touched the mark he'd left behind. "Sorry."

Laurence's hand covered his, imprisoning it to hold close to his skin. "I wasn't telling you to stop," he pointed out tenderly. "Are you a biter?"

Josh rolled his lips together, then nodded. "Yeah." He sighed, staring at the bruise forming on pale skin. "I've tried to curb it but—"

Laurence covered his mouth with a flat hand. "Don't you dare." He narrowed piercing blue eyes. "Who told you to change?"

Josh shrugged. Laurence raised his hand, but Josh knew he still had to answer. "Girls don't like being marked, and I don't blame them. It's hard to control."

Laurence ran patient fingers through Josh's hair. "Do me a favor, okay?"

Josh liked the fact that Laurence was still touching him. "Okay. Sure."

"Never change who you are. *Never*. Understood?"

"Uhh. Okay." Confusion tightened his features. "But—"

The hand that slapped over his mouth wasn't quite as gentle the second time. Laurence hung right over him, hard eyes giving no quarter. "First, I'm not a girl. Thought we had that ironed out long before now. Second, I repeat, I wasn't asking you to stop. Third, if the worry is that it will make me look slutty, then it's my worry, and frankly, Scarlet, I don't give a damn. Nod if you understand to this point."

Josh nodded, his pulse pounding in his ears. This was a side of Laurence he'd never known existed. It excited him. *He* excited Josh. Not many faced down Josh for anything.

"Good. Last, at least for the moment, I don't let just anyone brand the bull. So take it for what it is. You asked something of me this morning. Consider the fact that I'm now wearing your 'brand' my agreement."

Josh had to sift quickly through everything they'd discussed, trying to remember if it was that morning or last night as he replayed snips. Then... "No more hookups?"

"You're asking for exclusivity when we're not even in a relationship, you know that, right?" A single eyebrow arched over a knowing eye.

Josh opened his mouth then shut it. A long moment of silence stretched out between them. It hit him square when he realized exactly what Laurence had done with a single question. *Damn, he's good.* Laurence had just artfully tripped Josh face first through a door he'd still been checking the doorknob on to determine whether or not he was ready for everything Laurence brought with him. There were innumerable changes involved, questions he had and no answers. It was exactly like being a virgin all over again. And he had no choice but to go through with it. He'd requested the stipulation. Laurence was agreeing. Just on his own terms.

Silently, Josh applauded him. Very, very silently. "Sneaky, aren't you?"

"*Moi*? Don't have any idea what you mean."

With an unexpected tug of the fingers wound through silky hair, Josh claimed his lips, kissing him through his shock until he melted into Josh's frame. Josh really liked how it felt, liked the sinewy way their frames bent and shaped to each other's. Not soft and yielding like a woman's, but different and turning him on in a way women had ceased to months before. He'd never even known what he was missing.

He let Laurence go after the kiss, but only so far. "The hell you don't," Josh growled. He managed the next statement without wavering and a lot of bravado, no matter how hard his heart thundered in his ribs, riddled with uncertainty. "This *is* a relationship, and yes, exclusivity. Just...be patient. You've had years to be you. As of—" he rolled his head to the side to read the digital display on his clock "—not quite ten hours ago, I realized I cared for you and did something about it." Which, for lack of a better explanation, he guessed made Josh gay.

Laurence smirked. "Like punched out Ted's lights?"

"That was only because he lied to you, used you. I was leaving because I couldn't stand to see you with him any longer."

Josh noticed the awed surprise when it warmed Laurence, lightening his expression. It made him hate himself for what he was about to ask, but he had to know. "Did you have sex with him?"

Laurence traced Josh's ear with light fingertips. "No."

Josh was trying to figure it out, studying a calm Laurence. "Then what did you do?" *What did two guys do together?*

"Blow jobs, and I always use a condom. I don't give up my ass for hookups like that." Laurence paused his stroking. "I'm not *that* easy."

Josh held him by the chin, keeping him still to say, "Didn't think you were, but this is all brand new to me."

Laurence shifted again, a fleeting frown on his brow. "Josh," he began with a faint kiss to the hand that cradled him. "Can I go take a shower? This is getting uncomfortable."

"Of course. Want me to wash your clothes?"

"Could you?" Laurence asked. Relief curled his lips up. "I'm kinda glad you're not flipping out over this. I mean, you just made out—"

Josh covered his mouth this time. "Don't push it."

Laughter shook his frame, that intense glitter in the wild blue of his eyes making them seem livelier than ever. A mumbled, "Yes, sir," was heard.

"Just leave your clothes on the sink. I'll find something you can wear for when you get out."

Laurence nodded his agreement. Josh would shower after him. He was feeling the need himself. Though as Laurence slipped away and sauntered to the bathroom, his sculpted rear and all the parts above and below in plain sight, the imagined picture of Laurence under the spray and wet made his breathing quicken.

How did this happen? Josh couldn't look away until the door closed. Then he plopped flat to the bed with a heartfelt groan.

CHAPTER TWELVE

LAURENCE USED the toilet then quickly stripped, grimacing at the mess. "Rutting like animals," he chastised himself. Josh wasn't the only one who hadn't done that in a long time. Usually he had *some* control. Apparently, just not with Josh. After folding his clothes, he left them on the sink for Josh, like he asked. In front of the mirror, he caught his reflection. His neck was red and raw from Josh's beard, and right on the top of his shoulder was the hickey. Who knew being bitten was such a turn on? It had been years since he allowed anyone to give him one. He touched it, testing the tenderness. A shiver slid down his spine as memories of how he'd received it returned. He dropped his hand as if he'd been burned.

He slid the heavy curtain out of the way and started the water. "Oh yay," he murmured with a broad grin, taking in the powerful shower jet. "Come to daddy." He stepped in and glided under the spray, shivering in delight.

Finding the soap, he lathered up, immediately picturing Josh as the scent filled the humid space. He closed his eyes, the flash of skin and the feel of chest hair zipping through his thoughts. It was rough and soft at the same time. He loved running his fingers through it. Laurence sighed, washing and rinsing his bits with light hands. He was a little sore from the abuse this morning, but it wouldn't last long. Josh wasn't shy about getting what he wanted. The man was powerful. He moaned, thinking about how that would feel if they ever had sex. The strong snap of his hips, the ride of—

"Laurence?"

He froze under the water, feeling heat on his cheeks for being busted in his thoughts. "Josh?" he queried in the same tone.

Josh snorted, the nervousness leaking out of his voice. "Your things are in the wash and I have your keys. They must've fell out when you were in bed. I know it'll be big, but I found something for you."

The quiet snap of the door told him Josh was gone without being able to reply, or invite him into the shower. He wondered if Josh would have been up to it. Staring down, Laurence was more than up for it.

"Down, slick. We've gotten this far. He may still panic." Turning his face into the water, he let it flow over him. Taking a few more minutes, he washed his hair and by the time he was done, his body had calmed down.

After enjoying the pulsating tattoo of the water jet, he shut it off. Out of the tub, he dried skin and hair then spotted a toothbrush on top of a folded blue bundle on the sink. He smiled at the toothbrush. Josh was just a nice guy, when he wasn't being a jerk, he mused. Lifting the fabric, it turned out to be a pair of drawstring jogging shorts. At least with the string he could get them nearly snug. He twitched his hips to see how loose they were and laughed. *Jiggle it, baby.*

With those on, he brushed his teeth. "Now if I could find a brush, I'd feel human." He ran stiff fingers through his hair, loosening the damp clumps.

He blew himself a kiss in the mirror and walked out of the bathroom. He lazed in the living room from the couch's eye-view until Josh was done, scoping out Josh's apartment from his back. The couch was a butter cream leather beast, but still in great shape with a utilitarian oval table in front of it. There was a TV, and a small stereo under it. In general, the apartment was neat, for a bachelor pad, anyway. With a foot propped over a knee, he let his thoughts flit from one thing to another.

Laurence was still debating Josh's sanity by the time he appeared in the living room, freshly showered and looking just as edible as he had thirty minutes before. He'd changed as well, into a similar pair of shorts and nothing else. It was impossible not to look, or maybe just a necessity he couldn't ignore when he lowered his attention to a certain point below Josh's hips. And liked what he found. He imagined burying his nose into the hair coating his dick and wallowing in the scent. He loved how a man smelled, raw and musky.

"Hungry?" Josh asked, breaking into Laurence's appraisal.

Josh's gaze danced away when Laurence looked up at him. Laurence frowned and sat up. That wasn't right. "Josh?"

"Hm?" Josh walked into the small kitchen area and popped open the refrigerator to study the insides intently. "What are you hungry for?"

"How about a little truth?" Laurence was beginning to get a real bad feeling about all of this. Josh hadn't looked directly at him yet. Laurence crossed his arms on the fridge door and waited. Josh straightened reluctantly. Thick hair was towel-dry damp, and there wasn't a single hint of his thoughts in his eyes. Then again, he wasn't really looking toward him to be able to see what those thoughts could be. Laurence lifted his braced arms off the cold metal when Josh went to ease the door shut.

"Truth about what?"

Lowering his arms, Laurence took a step toward Josh. He retreated almost instantly.

"See! I knew it. You're already regretting this!" Laurence wasn't sure why that one action infuriated him so quickly.

"I'm not!" Josh looked around, a hint of desperation in the act. "What can I make you?"

"I don't want food right now." Laurence took another step closer and when Josh tried to run, he was stopped completely by the counter at his back. "Light of day, Josh. Tell me the truth."

He shook his head, not understanding. "What do you think all of that was in the bedroom?"

"Endorphins and feeling high from doing something naughty."

Josh's lips parted. A shock of air filled the quiet. His stuttered breathing. "No." He closed his eyes. "Damn it, Laurence. Don't push me."

"Why not? You have *pushed* me for four years. Pushed me away. Now I want the truth."

"Laurence, everything I've told you up to now has been the honest truth." There was no inflection, no steeled edge. It was as he said, if Laurence could believe him.

"So if I told you right now to kiss me, what would you do?"

Josh's shoulders relaxed. "Hopefully think it wasn't meant as a punishment because I've wanted to since you went to shower."

"You want to kiss me?" *Shit. He was serious?* It was almost incomprehensible for Laurence. "Then why did you back away from me? Why did you avoid me just now?" What the hell was going on in his head?

"Did you want me to come out of the bedroom and jump on you? Because in just those shorts, that is almost what happened. And I would have been absolutely happy with anything we did."

"So this isn't a test? A game?" Josh was tilting Laurence's world.

Josh physically relaxed. A hint of understanding warmed his eyes and his lips parted with a slight smile. "Believe me, it's taken me even longer to get here. And the answer is no and no. I'm not 'playing' at being gay. In all honesty, knowing how biology works, there probably is another man out there who I could feel something for." He held up his hand when Laurence scowled at him. "But see, I trust you, Laurence. I *know* you. And I hope you'll give me the chance to learn how to do this because I only *want* to do it with you."

Laurence fidgeted on the balls of his feet.

"And that is my truth. The question is, are you willing to do this with me?" He bent, cocking his head to peer at Laurence. When he remained quiet, Josh added, "You know, they say there's a thin line between love and hate."

"I've never hated you," Laurence quickly said.

"But I never made it easy for you to like me either."

Laurence took a small step in his direction and watched as Josh's eyes followed him, darkening. "So you think this is one of those 'friends to lovers' things?"

"Would it sound corny if I said I hope so?"

Laurence groaned with a touch of playful exasperation. "You're impossible."

Josh reached out for him and Laurence closed the remaining distance, holding his hand. Warmth rolled from their connected fingers up his arm. Josh's other raised and delicately traced and caressed the tender junction of Laurence's shoulder. "Is it wrong that just seeing this is turning me on?"

Laurence shivered. The hickey was sensitive, but even more so, Josh's caring touch was making his head spin. "I don't think so."

The desire growing between them almost snapped on the air. After years of seeing one thing, convincing himself that Josh hated him, was homophobic, wasn't willing to let his old prejudices go, here he stood, slowly turning Laurence to mush. What he found now in Josh made his heart gallop. He couldn't hide it or fight the way his body leaned toward Josh's frame. Like he was a divining rod, and Josh was the pull he sought.

Somehow, the last few centimeters vanished between them. Barefoot, Laurence reached his shoulder, Josh a full head taller. When Josh wound his arms around Laurence's body, he melted into his strength. On autopilot, a raised hand threaded through the hair on his chest, teasing and winding it over fingertips.

Josh sighed. "That tickles." His voice held that contented rumble that sank into Laurence like hot cocoa on a chilly morning.

Right after his shower, the scent of the soap, Josh's warm skin and the heat coursing beneath it filled Laurence's nose. He drew it deep into his lungs. Laurence could easily become addicted to that.

"Now, are you hungry?"

Laurence's eyes fluttered closed. Skin to skin, there wasn't anything else. Nothing else that mattered anyway. "Depends. Are you on the menu?"

"Me?" Josh stopped moving. Felt like he might have stopped breathing too.

"Well, we do have a whole weekend." Laurence captured Josh's floating hand, bringing it to his lips. With thorough care, he kissed the thin scratch scars on the back of it, making sure he got each one. The pads of Josh's fingers were rough in Laurence's palm, though not as calloused as they once had been. He shivered, remembering how those same fingers had felt against his skin, roaming his back.

"What are you doing?" Josh whispered.

Laurence stiffened his tongue to poke and lick between two fingers. Josh's breathing sped up. "Making you feel good."

Josh groaned when he lapped at the tip of a finger. The hand still wrapped around his body flexed.

"Is it working?" Laurence licked the flesh of the finger he held then slowly drew the entire digit into his mouth. Josh's physical reaction was definitely apparent. It was currently rubbing and twitching against his stomach through the cotton of Josh's running shorts.

"God, you're good at that," he said, sounding more and more raspy. His deep voice was doing wicked things to Laurence's insides. Josh's arm tightened around his back when Laurence sucked, riding the length of his finger to the end.

"Do you have condoms?"

Josh nodded, his eyes heavily lidded and storming gray.

"There's something you have that I'd much rather be doing this to."

"Oh, God." Josh shuddered. He hadn't looked away once.

When Laurence took a sliding step to guide him out of the kitchen, Josh followed.

CHAPTER THIRTEEN

JOSH TRIED not to stumble, even though he was short-circuiting between his brain and every other part of himself. He couldn't look away from Laurence's lips, pink and smooth sliding up and down his finger, now shiny and slick. His dick ached, watching him. Somehow they made it back into the bedroom. He didn't argue when Laurence gave him a gentle but firm guiding shove to lay on the bed.

"I really can't believe this is happening," Laurence said with a wispy breathlessness.

"Is it bad? You don't want—"

Laurence did that thing with his fingers again, pressing them to Josh's lips. He doubted the other man had even an inkling of how that got to Josh.

"Definitely not bad." Laurence crawled up on the bed. "My big, burly caveman." He nuzzled into Josh's chest.

Josh admired his length as Laurence played to his heart's content, roaming across his chest, running discovering lips over exposed skin. What he was doing left little doubt that Laurence was thoroughly enjoying his adventures. Soft purrs, light kisses, flicking licks and then... *"Oh, shit."* Josh hissed, flexing uncontrollably as sparks lit on his eyelids.

Laurence teased at his nipple, doing things with his mouth that made his eyes cross. "What... Oh, God. Laurence." Josh couldn't help himself. He threaded a hand through the tousle of fine, sunlight blond hair, needing to touch. Laurence's response was to rub a cheek to his chest like a contented cat. Then he returned to the torture that had been slowly melting Josh's brain.

None of the girls he'd dated had been particularly fond of the chest hair, so he'd never experienced the mind-numbing bliss Laurence was so easily giving him. He'd never known how good it felt to be licked and teased. Then Laurence migrated due west and repeated the delicious sensations.

Laurence used his tongue like a weapon, carving and slicing his body apart. Nerves tingled all over.

"Shit!" Josh jerked, groaning when Laurence dipped into his belly button.

"Too much?"

Josh couldn't speak, only rocking his head in answer.

"Remember, handsome. If anything is too much, stop me." He felt Laurence adjust, Josh's hand still loosely wound through the fall of his hair, following his motions until Laurence hung over him. "Look at me, Josh."

He cracked his eyes open with monumental effort. His entire body was singing the praises of Laurence's mouth. He didn't mentally trip in the least, knowing it was Laurence either. Not with those amazing blue eyes piercing him all the way to his soul.

"I want you to enjoy this. Want you to feel good, because I feel good doing it for you, but if anything is too much, say so."

Peering up into his earnest eyes, waiting for a single sign of approval and agreement, Josh's heart skipped. "Want you to." He wasn't sure when or if he'd ever be able to do the same, but for right now, Laurence was playing him as skillfully as any violinist. Then to add his own level of proof, he brought Laurence close and kissed him. Licked at his lips for entry then danced over his tongue. Teasing at Laurence, he snagged the tip of his tongue between light teeth and drew on it, suckling. Laurence's entire length shivered and he moaned, a soft keening sound that drove right through Josh's heart.

Slowly, he let him go, still stunned at how much he enjoyed that, how much he wanted more, and by how much he hoped Laurence never stopped.

"Where are the rubbers?"

Josh gulped for air. He didn't know exactly *what* Laurence had in mind, but he knew he could hold him to his word that at any point he'd back off. He also realized to what depth he truly trusted the man gazing at him. "Bathroom. By the towels."

Laurence coasted over his chin with kisses. "Stay right there."

Josh couldn't have moved even if the bed was on fire. Okay, maybe for that, but anything else? Didn't even enter his radar. He watched Laurence's swish as he vanished into the bathroom to return a moment later. The tent in the front of his shorts sent electric chills down Josh.

Laurence opened his hand and dumped several condoms on the nightstand. He climbed with a seductive prowl onto the bed, his pale eyes pinned on Josh. "You are incredible," Laurence murmured. He lowered and licked at the soft skin of Josh's inner thigh.

Josh fisted the covers when Laurence bent close and buried his nose in the vee of his legs. Trembles shot to every corner at the playful tease of his hot tongue. Without knowing what drove him, he widened his straddle and was rewarded almost instantly. A tremulous sigh escaped Laurence when he bent close again and this time that wicked tongue licked over his balls.

"No underwear. Sexy as hell, caveman." Laurence's weight shifted as he knelt on the bed. "Can I take these off you now?"

Josh trembled but not out of fear. He hooked one side and getting the signal, Laurence eased fingers into the elastic on his hip and together they shimmied them down. Bending his legs to help, Laurence peeled them off Josh and tossed them.

"Could lick you for days." Laurence sighed in rapt pleasure.

"Yeah?" Josh see-sawed between wanting to melt and wanting to combust. Those words were of the melting variety.

Lashes dipped, hiding Laurence's eyes. "I've always thought you were hot, Josh."

Josh sat up, his body bending in the middle. Gently grasping Laurence in his palms, he kissed him, a bone-melting, mind-bending kiss of Josh-sized proportions. When he let Laurence go, they were both trembling. "I'm yours." He bit off the "baby" that wanted to come naturally to his lips. He wasn't sure if it was right, or wanted, but he did know that what they were sharing was better than perfection.

Laurence pressed him back to the bed. He obeyed without a fight.

"Do I get to see you?" Josh whispered.

"You want me naked?" Laurence paused with his hand on Josh's chest.

Rolling his bottom lip between his teeth, hoping he wasn't doing yet something else wrong, he nodded. "All of you."

Laurence's eyes closed and a shiver rocked his shoulders. Josh wanted to touch and all that separated him was a pair of shorts from his deepest desires. For years, he'd been unable to ignore the pert little butt, the smooth roundness of perfection in those damn jeans or pressed pants that he wore when he was working with other students. He'd touched it once that morning, held Laurence in the palm of his hand, but now, he wanted...however much he could manage, however much he thought he could offer.

Laurence slipped from the bed one more time. Standing at the edge, he unknotted the drawstring. The waist sat right below his hips, hanging low with a dare at his hipbones. Then they were falling. And Josh was staring at a naked man. An utterly incredible naked man.

"God, you're beautiful."

Laurence stood there, letting him take his fill. Laurence's waist was cut, his stomach flat and his chest smooth. Narrow hips were aligned with slightly broader shoulders. Lean and long legs were muscled. He was as perfect as a sculpture. Even the fine hair at his groin was perfect, a shade darker than his hair, but what grabbed Josh by the throat until his mouth went dry was the cock sticking up and bobbing oh-so-gently at him. His wasn't terribly thick, but the length... *Oh fuck*. Josh moaned taking it all in, all of the man and all his parts.

Mine. It was a silent growl of possession, happened and was gone before it solidified. He'd think about it later.

"Still okay?" Laurence's soft words dragged his focus up. Patient eyes watched him.

"No."

Josh saw the dejection, the cave of his shoulders when Laurence deflated. And the flash of hurt.

Before he could bend to retrieve his shorts, Josh said clearly, "You're not on this bed with me."

Laurence straightened with a shocked burst. Josh raised a hand to him. Tentatively, Laurence threaded their fingers together. Running his hand over Laurence's side, he eased Laurence onto the bed with him. He only got as far as lying directly over and above Josh. His body sung with the surge of heat between them.

Laurence lowered his weight and they were skin to skin. Josh's fingers flexed where he held Laurence's side.

Josh blinked. "Does it always feel like this?" he whispered. A sense of rightness, of awe swarmed over him as he absorbed it all.

"Like what, Josh?" Laurence was stroking, soothing, tender fingers creating furrows through his hair.

"Like I want to be like this, be a part of you and stay there?"

Laurence stared at him and said nothing. Josh swallowed. His pulse beat with an echo that began to get louder and louder.

When Laurence finally spoke, Josh was seconds from a panic attack, from ending it all and never looking back at his most foolish mistake.

"It's perfect, Josh." Laurence flattened himself to Josh like a second skin. The contours of body meshed and mirrored. Hard muscle to hard muscle. Each breath eased them together like ships on the tide, flesh to flesh. "Want you." Laurence's whispered words were raw and reached deep into Josh.

Josh knew that longing, understood the wanting. Holding Laurence within his arms, it was as though four years of insecurity, misunderstandings, anger and fear melted away. There was now. Them, together.

Nothing in his life had ever felt more right. Josh turned his head, his lips brushing against Laurence's ears with the wisp of a breeze. "Show me." A fresh shudder rolled down Laurence. Something Josh had never felt in his life, the silken slide of a dick against his, the friction of skin to skin stole his breath. Laurence moaned, his fingers digging into Josh's hair.

Lips slid down Josh's throat, the damp heat of a wicked tongue wrapping his desires and tying them into a neat bow. A rumbled sigh filled the quiet of the bedroom. Then Laurence was moving, kissing, sucking, nibbling and teasing. Soon, he'd slid beyond Josh's reach though he never stopped touching.

The slick heat of Laurence's tongue against his balls arched his spine. With his eyes closed, sparks danced across his vision. Laurence drew on one and rolled it over his tongue. Josh moaned, oblivious to everything but the intense pleasure rising upward from that wicked, talented mouth. When Laurence blew across damp skin, Josh almost jerked out of his skin.

"Oh, God." He gasped. No one had ever made him feel like this.

Then Laurence upped the stakes. He dragged the flat of his tongue up the length of his shaft, pressing on the vein underneath. Josh's head rocked side to side. "Fuck! Laurence." His chest heaved.

"Taste so good," Laurence purred, licking around and up and down.

Josh knew it was wrong to compare him to the women he'd slept with. Laurence was in a league by himself. It was clearly apparent that the pleasure Laurence was giving was also being taken, that Laurence wanted to lick and touch as much as he knew Josh wanted it.

"Laurence," he rasped. He was getting close, his balls tightening and tingling as the need for release grew.

"Shh. I got you." Laurence stroked his thigh, running fingers through the short hairs of his groin. "Better?" he asked a moment later when Josh wasn't panting like a freight train.

He gulped and nodded. His mind was zeroed in on every caress and touch. Then Laurence shifted and the rip of a condom opening showered him with goose bumps. "Okay, sexy. Just relax."

Josh couldn't have moved if he'd wanted to.

The press of the condom rolling down his length startled him and he lifted enough to focus on what Laurence was doing. Slim fingers guided it to the base, giving him light squeezes.

"Remember your finger?" Laurence asked.

Josh managed a croaked, "Yeah."

When Laurence rose above him on his knees, Josh got a clue. "Oh fuck!" He growled, a hoarse shout. Wet heat covered the tip of his cock. "Shit, Laurence. Fuck. Yesss!" He ground his hands into the bedding, his hips lurching. Laurence swallowed him as deep as he could. Moving up and down in a slow ride was Josh's undoing. It had been too long since he'd enjoyed any type of contact.

He thrust and Laurence opened wide and took it. The wind of silky hair twisted over his fingers, though he never remembered lifting his arm.

"Shit, yes! So good. So...*ughnn*...fucking hot." Words grew to unintelligible mumbles and growls. The swipe of a tongue, the hard press of jaws and Josh cried out, erupting into the condom with an orgasm that ripped upward from his toes. Heat roared down his spine from his nape.

Laurence moaned, the vibration sinking through latex and skin, skittering shivers across Josh in a cascade of shocks. The sweet pressure of his mouth milked him through to the end, until Josh was a mess of bones and skin on the bed and not much else.

Laurence eventually pulled off the condom and tied it to dispose of. He kissed Josh's hip. "Be right back." He eased from the bed for the bathroom.

The sound of running water reached the bed, then he returned with a damp towel. He cleaned up Josh's softened length, drying him tenderly. Once on the bed, he swiped at the covers and Josh realized Laurence had also... He swallowed.

"Did you?"

He grimaced apologetically. "Hard. Sorry for the mess." He dabbed at Josh's leg and Josh chuckled. He hadn't even noticed, he'd been so mind blown with his own orgasm.

"Shut up." He smiled sleepily at Laurence, catching the bright red on his cheeks. "Clean enough," Josh decreed, not wanting to wait any longer to hold him again. "Toss that and come 'ere." He was drowsy, slurring his words. He widened an arm and Laurence snuggled into his side. "Amazing, baby."

"Baby?"

Shit! Totally missed catching it that time. Josh tensed but a soothing hand petted circles on his chest.

"It's okay, handsome. I like hearing it from you."

Josh melted. A few minutes later, he rolled to his side and Laurence flipped, scooting to press back to chest. Josh wrapped caging arms around his body and was out like a light.

CHAPTER FOURTEEN

LAURENCE KNEW he was in deep shit. Lying in Josh's arms, snuggled against the heater that was his body, he didn't want to move. Maybe not ever.

So not good. Though that was the problem. It was fucking perfect. Josh was considerably taller but they were skin to skin like two peas.

He wasn't sure what time it was. It had to be late morning by the slant of light coming into the bedroom. Not that it really mattered. He wasn't in any kind of a hurry to leave the bed or the man in it. Something he rarely did was stay, either overnight or for any length of time. With a grimace, the night before and Ted cycled in front of his vision. Definitely not with him. Wouldn't have even if he had been drunk, which he hadn't been. Ted couldn't and didn't compare to Josh. Laurence had held no idea that he was playing with dynamite the night before by hooking up with Ted.

Josh had always had his back. He just hadn't seen it through the years for what it was. *Forest, trees et al,* he supposed. Josh had always been skittish, and even rude on occasion. What else was Laurence supposed to think? It was coming to terms with the *he doesn't hate me* vibe that was harder than he'd thought it would be. He guessed he was still waiting for the shoe to drop, or for Josh to wake up and realize just what was going on.

A rumbled sigh filtered into the room from behind him and he caressed the arm slung over his waist. Crisp hair tickled his fingers. Where Laurence was light and blond, Josh was darker all around. A brown so dark, his hair appeared nearly black, gray eyes that could stop Laurence's heart from beating or make it race, a rich, sun-bronzed hint of tan to his skin and muscles that screamed his strength.

Engrossed in his comparisons, he traced the thin white-ish scars on the back of the hand before him with a light touch.

"Just what kind of ranching does your dad do?" he asked quietly, not wanting to shatter the companionable quiet.

"He raises beef cattle. Beefmaster and Highland cattle. He only keeps a couple hundred of each through the breeding season."

"And you didn't get an agricultural management degree?"

"I love my parents, and I don't hate what they do, but it's not what I want to do." Josh drew him closer, tightening the band of his arm around Laurence. The bed was warm and soft, though they never made it beneath the sheets this morning. "We had a very long discussion when I was sixteen or so. I'm grateful and probably a lot luckier than many. My parents have always let me find my own roads. They would have loved it if I'd followed in their footsteps, but I knew it wasn't a deep love for me like it is for them. They live and breathe ranching and bovine husbandry."

"What will happen to the land and cattle?"

"When it gets to be too much, he already has a buyer for it. An older, established farming and ranching brand. He said he'll talk to me again before he goes through with anything."

"But that's like a family legacy," Laurence interjected.

"It'll be a while," Josh said with a comforting caress of his chin to the top of Laurence's head. "They're both barely in their forties. I was a high school prom night whoops."

"Oh, wow!" Laurence threaded his fingers through the top of Josh's hand, twining them together.

Josh chuckled in agreement. "And they're still as nuts about each other as they were at eighteen."

"That's sweet."

Josh shifted along his back and ran a hand down Laurence's arm. "You're not cold, are you?"

"No."

"I'm going to make something to eat and get the clothes out of the dryer." He nuzzled Laurence's ear. Laurence's eyes sank shut fast with the bare caress of lips. He most definitely was not cold. "Sound good to you?"

"Mm hm," he murmured, arching into the whisper of skin against his ear.

"Behave." Josh nipped lightly without teeth. "It's hard enough having you naked in bed with me."

Laurence stiffened just as Josh let him go, climbing out of bed. *Hard enough? Hard enough how?* Was Josh already distancing himself? Was he beginning to have doubts? Laurence rolled to the nearest edge of the bed, only to realize the shorts he'd worn earlier were by Josh.

The bed rocked beneath him and he waited for Josh to leave the room so he could dress without a witness to his humiliation. He wondered what would be the fastest route out the front door to reach his car. He knew he was going to regret this. Josh wasn't gay.

"Laurence?" Arms wrapped around his shoulders. The bed dipped when Josh knelt behind him.

Escape blocked.

"Josh?" he replied.

Josh chuckled, pressing his lips to Laurence's shoulder, the mark that still tingled, hours later. Slowly, Josh's mouth cruised up his neck, swirling his talented tongue along the tendon.

"Look, Josh." Laurence steeled himself. He didn't want to fight about it. He only wanted to get out as unscathed as he could. He knew he was already in way over his head.

Josh hesitated in his oral roaming. "What?"

"I don't think I can do this," Laurence whispered, staring at a speck of sunlight on the carpet.

"What? Why?" Josh managed, choking on the words and sounding like he was trying to swallow marbles.

"Because in a few hours, a few days, you're going to realize this isn't what you want—"

Laurence cried out when he was jerked backward onto the bed, a scowling Josh hanging directly over him. "How many times do I have to go over this?" His expression was darkening, any show of patience absent. "I've been repeating the same damn thing since last night. What do you want from me? A declaration of love? I'm sorry. I can't do that, but that doesn't mean I won't. Want me to suck you like a Hoover? Fine, bring that bad boy up here. Sex is sex, Laurence, but I wouldn't even be doing this if I didn't think there was a chance for something between us. If all I wanted was a fast fuck, there's like five women I could call and they'd drop everything to be with me."

"Aha! Women," Laurence barked, only to wince when Josh slapped the bed.

"Want to know why *only* women?" he retorted scathingly, glaring at him through those stormy gray eyes. "Because the only man I want is already in my bed, but he's convinced I'm going to wake up like this is some strange dream. Aren't you? Go ahead, say it. You think I'm playing."

"No, not playing," Laurence tried, biting at his lip. "But—"

"No. There is no 'but' to this, Laurence. Want to know why Timmy turned me on? Because he reminded me of you. Want to know why the last two girls I dated were blonde? Because they reminded me of you. Want to know why I'd call a woman? Because it would *only* be a fuck." He growled and bounced a little on bent arms, a mid-rise push-up. "You. Just you. You drive me insane. You're so damned hot, the prettiest man I've ever known. I love the way your body moves. Christ, it's like you're walking with your own Samba beat. Drives me up a damned wall."

Laurence's eyes rounded.

"Now, you tell me? Are *you* going to stick this out? So I'm not a gay man with a hundred name list. Frankly, I don't even have that many women on the list. This is more than you thinking I'm going to play 'gotcha'. You think I'm planning this, or you're too damned scared to find out if this is even possible, because it *could* be something special."

Laurence quickly shook his head. "No! I know it's not that."

Josh stared hard at him for several tense heartbeats, then he swung an arm over Laurence's chest and sank down, effectively pinning him. The pounding tattoo of his heart shot through Josh's chest to vibrate Laurence. "So this is the deal, gorgeous. I agreed to your monogamy of a relationship. You agree that this is happening. No going back. No more 'is he going to wake up' doubts. No more throwing the damned gauntlet. If you don't want to be here with me, that's one thing. I won't force you, but if these issues are only because I seem to have switched teams when you don't think it's possible, then nothing I've said up 'til now has even made it into that brain of yours."

Laurence panted, Josh's weight bearing down on him, holding him as mercilessly as any chain. He barely dared to blink.

"So it really is me," he whispered, searching. "Just me?"

"Just you, Laurence." Josh inched closer. "It's always been just you."

"Pretty?" His tongue moistened his bottom lip, unsure but not wanting to rile Josh again.

A dull red snuck onto Josh's cheeks above his beard line. He didn't avoid or try to drop Laurence's searching gaze when he explained it. "Yes. Not feminine, but pretty. Everything from your pale hair to your eyes. Your lips. Soft skin." Josh's words were losing the volatile heat of his outburst. "I didn't see myself as gay before meeting you..."

Josh glared when Laurence's mouth popped open and he meekly closed it.

"I'd never known anyone like you, either." Josh lightly toyed with a few strands of hair between his fingers. "I'm not going to repeat everything again, so just nod, and tell me you're moving past this, because honestly, I'm starving, and I'm also getting turned on. So if we don't eat, we are going to be doing a lot more on this bed in the very immediate future."

"Can we do more after we eat?" Laurence asked hopefully, praying Josh heard the apology for doubting him in it.

When Josh lowered and kissed him until he couldn't breathe, he had his answer.

CHAPTER FIFTEEN

IN THE QUIET of the courtyard between the Tech building and two others, Josh read through another page, making notes and giving encouragement when he saw the student had gone above the curve on his report. This particular topic wasn't part of his intended curriculum for his own degree, but he needed the Assistant hours. The more he worked with the drafting and design professors, the more he enjoyed the challenges. Coding and systems, hardware and programs. Refocusing on the page before him, a little science never hurt anyone, but he was certainly glad he wasn't leaning toward physics for himself, which was the current stack of entry-level papers Dr. Lench had given him that morning to read over.

"Mr. Daily?"

Interrupted out of his reading, Josh looked up at the young man at his shoulder. "Can I help you?" He wasn't a student that he knew, but Josh swore he looked familiar. He was in his early twenties with brown hair and sparkling eyes. A beige and black backpack hung off a shoulder.

Slim fingers held out a small ivory linen envelope. "Mr. Broker asked me to deliver this for him."

"Mr. Broker? Professor Broker?" Josh straightened. Why would Professor Broker be inviting him to something? And to what? They weren't even in the same buildings and he taught a completely different subject matter. In other words, not even in the same league. He didn't think they'd ever met face to face either.

A whimsical smile and a nod were his answer. "You may remember him, sir. Sean Broker."

Josh's eyes opened clearly. "Club Six? *That* was Professor Sean Broker that night?" It was a good thing he was sitting. That man was worth a fortune and gave hundreds of thousands to the university every year. His studies on gravity and the effects and possibilities of black holes in space were well documented. Professor Broker had been quoted and exalted numerous times in several studies done by NASA. And he had been at Club Six. No wonder Sean knew he wasn't a regular there. He *knew* who Josh was even if Josh hadn't a clue that night. The envelope didn't waver.

The young man's face lit up with energy at Josh's recognition. "Please accept the invitation. He would be so delighted if you could join him."

Josh slid the envelope from waiting fingers into his own. Placing the young man who stood before him now, he wracked his memory, hoping he was matching the name to the face correctly. "Misha?"

The young man's face beamed even more with pleasure. "Yes, sir! Master hopes you will join him for dinner."

Master? Josh's curiosity was definitely getting the better of him.

Misha's phone beeped from a pocket. "Oh! That's my alarm. I have to get to class. It was a pleasure seeing you again, Mr. Daily."

"You too, Misha," Josh responded, though unsure. He watched until the young man's trim form was swallowed up by other students entering the building. Blinking, he realized he still held the envelope in his hand.

Popping the seal on the back—an honest to God pressed hot wax seal—he withdrew the folded card from the envelope and read.

Please do me the honor of accepting this invitation for dinner. A guest is welcome and encouraged.
R.S.V.P.

The date, phone number and house address were also written in the flowing cursive. Why was he inviting Josh to dinner? And who could he take? Thinking of their meeting at Club Six, and talking with Misha, he doubted a woman would be comfortable under the circumstances. Sean obviously lived slightly out of the expected norm. *Then who?*

Sliding the envelope into one of his carry case side pockets, he returned to the papers on the table, though the haunting ghost of the invitation was never far from his thoughts.

LAURENCE PICKED at the white napkin beneath his silverware with antsy fingers. He glanced up every time a person walked into the café through the wide glass doors, then smiled weakly when RJ spotted him. RJ cleared the distance between tables with ease.

"I didn't take you from a new client, did I?"

RJ sat down, shaking his head. "No, but I do need to go look at a possible office. If I get it, I'll have to hire someone."

"You're really getting off the ground with this, aren't you?" Laurence perked up, beaming for RJ's success.

RJ relaxed, crossing a leg over the other under the table. "I can't believe it myself. Who knew what knowing the difference between ecru and ivory could do for your reputation."

Laurence chuckled when RJ snickered. Laurence knew it was more than that. RJS Events was RJ's baby now, a full service event and theme planner, and while he didn't enjoy weddings, he managed them with every bit as much *savoir-faire* as the next contract. A couple well-placed opportunities that he'd handled with more than gentle hands, professionalism and taste had been one of the best things to happen to Laurence's best friend.

"Maybe you leaving school wasn't the worst thing," he offered. "Not if you're doing this well with it." He refused to let his own angst and sorrow at not having RJ near bring him down. For the first time since RJ's predicaments began, he looked settled, relaxed and genuinely happy.

RJ met his gaze boldly, then after a moment, let out a breath and glanced away. "I know. We all have to make our own way, right?" Laurence didn't point out the regret RJ couldn't hide.

Laurence knew maybe better than most what RJ had to sacrifice. He still didn't know it all, and probably didn't know nearly enough. He hadn't pried, but had let RJ know he was there for him when the shit hit the fan.

A waiter approached and they requested their drinks, taking menus and glancing at them briefly.

Laurence wasn't sure he'd even be able to eat. His entire world had been kicked onto its ass end over the previous weekend. Choosing a light sandwich, he squeezed lemon into his water and gave it a sample taste. RJ handed his menu over, making his request and then they were left alone again.

"Oh, dear. This *is* one of those lunches, isn't it?" RJ asked sympathetically now.

"What do you mean?" Laurence asked, confused.

"You only drink lemon water when you're at odds."

Laurence sat up on his seat. "What are you talking about?"

"I heard it in your voice this morning." RJ leaned forward, resting an elbow on the table to prop his chin on. "Okay, talk to me."

Laurence studied one of his closest friends, wondering why RJ had never appealed to him. Life would have been so much simpler if he had. RJ was out, self-assured, ambitious, not to mention strikingly handsome with gorgeous soft black hair to his collar and gray eyes, though a little lighter than Josh's.

Josh.

He dropped his focus to the napkin again. "I think I'm in trouble."

"Oh, honey!" RJ reached for one of his hands. "What is it? Were you arrested?"

Laurence dissuaded that assumption right away. "No, nothing illegal." Rising to take in the countenance across from him, he whispered, "It's Josh."

"Shit, what did that ape do now?" RJ griped with annoyance. "Doesn't he get his jollies enough without dragging you into crap?"

"No! It's not like that."

"He treats you like shit. Why do you let him get to you?"

"Because he is a friend to all of us," he countered, narrowing his eyes. "He's been coming around." He paraphrased what Gregory had said oh so many moons ago. Biting his lip, he was beginning to wonder if he should even discuss it. He knew RJ was only trying to protect him, taking his side because he'd witnessed the torment that Josh had heaped on him. To be fair, Laurence had done his share as well. He wasn't defenseless, and he sure wasn't guiltless either.

"And I've seen how he treats you. He is our friend, but you two should not be allowed in the same room alone together."

Laurence slid his hand away from RJ's to let his friend sit comfortably, hiding his wince while he was at it at RJ's rejoinder.

"I was with him at Club Six." Laurence knew that with RJ not around the group he hadn't witnessed Josh's lighter attitude, the protective stance he invariably carried whenever Laurence was around. Looking back over the last few encounters, he was surprised to see it clearly, and even more disappointed in himself that he hadn't recognized what Josh had been conveying when he hadn't found the words. A touch here, a small gesture there. There were more ways than words to show a person how they felt. And Laurence had missed them all.

RJ was quick to point out Laurence's faults, even though it wasn't meant as a criticism. "No. You hooked up with the first cock to look your way."

Laurence pursed his lips. He had, and damn, had he regretted it too.

Their waiter arrived with their plate lunches and after a quick check for more, he left them alone to eat.

Laurence waited for RJ to not be chewing or drinking before dropping the next bomb.

"I spent the weekend with him." He ducked quickly and popped a large morsel into his mouth.

"What?" RJ froze, his fork in midair, his jaw dropped open.

Laurence gulped, a hard dry effort. A sip of water didn't help much. "Just hear me out, okay?"

RJ agreed by setting his fork on the edge of his plate. "Enlighten me," he deadpanned.

"After we left Club Six...I took him to my place to clean his hand. He'd cut it on dickhead's tooth." Laurence actually hoped Josh had knocked a few loose after the lies he'd told Laurence.

RJ settled back into his chair, his arms crossed over his chest.

Laurence pushed another bite of bread around with a fingertip. "He kissed me."

"He was drunk."

Laurence didn't bother to get into that argument. He knew the truth. "He wasn't at four Saturday morning."

"What the fuck, Laurence?"

He flinched. "I was confused!" he all but wailed. Looking around, the bustle of the café afforded them some privacy. People were eating and talking, and in no way interested to their table by the wall. "He kissed me out of the blue and left before I could react."

"Probably a good thing," RJ muttered. "There were no knives nearby, I hope?"

"RJ!" he growled.

RJ leaned forward, bracing a finger on the table. "Look, Josh is a great guy. We both know how he feels about gay people. He's our friend in spite of it. I can only guess how hard of a stretch it is for him. There are some straight people that I deal with, and it's with a certain level of restraint."

"So you don't think all the hate could be denial?" Laurence's voice was a bare sound, his own doubts tripling in size. It wasn't like he hadn't assumed the same conclusions since that first kiss. The discussion—or arguments—since had been ricocheting through his head. Was it possible for Josh to really mean it? *Could* he be gay after all? What about the last four years? The years before he even knew Laurence? He knew Josh had girlfriends. There was no mistaking that in his history. There was also the impassioned Josh of the weekend, making his case and why.

Laurence wished he knew how to spot the truth.

RJ scooped up his fork and took a bite. A moment later, he said, "The question is, do *you* think it could be denial?"

Laurence swallowed heavily. "I honestly don't think he wants to hurt me." He couldn't say it out loud, but given the new view of Josh, Laurence had to admit he liked what he saw. A lot. It definitely hadn't felt like Josh was playing. He'd sworn that strongly himself. Josh knew his own mind. Laurence hoped that was the case.

He hadn't spent a weekend like he had with Josh, ever. They lounged. They ate. They played, in and out of bed. They even talked. Laurence had hated to see the end of the weekend. Now if that wasn't a first.

"Really? Josh? What happened to the fists of fury? You two don't speak unless it's a fight."

Laurence ripped off a piece of his sandwich and popped it between his lips. "Oh, believe me, there was that too, but..." He ran his finger over the rim of his water glass. "Am I insane for even giving him the chance?"

"You're sounding like a girl," RJ teased, though his smile was lighter.

Laurence shrugged, unrepentant.

"Just...be careful. He's not gay."

He couldn't help the frown RJ's declaration raised because Laurence feared RJ was more right than Josh was.

CHAPTER SIXTEEN

JOSH HELD the invitation in his fingers. Taking a breath, he lifted the phone on the bedside table. When the ringing began, he almost hung up out of self-preservation. He wasn't even that sure of just what he was terrified of, whether Laurence would say yes, no, or why he wanted Laurence to go to begin with.

"Hello?"

Josh drew a breath, unsure how Laurence would feel now that there was time since the revelations of the weekend. "Hi, Laurence. Are you busy?" Committed, he placed the card near the phone.

"Nope. Scrambling up some dinner."

Josh couldn't remember ever being this nauseous asking out a woman. "Do you have plans Thursday night?"

Silence filled the space between them.

"No." Laurence's voice was soft, with a hint of surprise floating in there too.

"Would you like to go somewhere with me?" Josh put a hand over his face. *Fuck. Just ask him!*

"Josh, are you asking me out? A date?"

Grow a pair! He licked his lips, then firmed his voice and his resolve. "I am. A dinner with a professor from the university."

"Josh," Laurence replied with hesitant slowness. "Are you sure? Wouldn't a woman date be...more appropriate?"

Josh relaxed when that was his argument, not that he didn't want to, couldn't go, at all. "In this case, not in the least." He also realized while saying that he would never go anywhere with a woman to escort again. Stag or with Laurence. Josh was fine with that. "It's not formal or anything," Josh explained. "Don't wear your clubbing shirt." He snickered when Laurence huffed on the other end.

"Which professor?"

"Professor Broker, Astrological Physics."

"Oh wow! I know who he is."

"Have you met him?" Josh asked, his curiosity piqued.

Laurence hummed into the phone and brought goose bumps to Josh's flesh. "Not face to face, no. Heard he's brilliant, though."

"I have an invitation for Thursday, and want you to go with me." *Please.* Perched on the bed, he held his breath, waiting.

"Josh. I— I—" Tension was making Josh tremble as he waited for the letdown. "Okay. Yes."

Josh's heart pounded back to life, knowing Laurence had been working a way into declining. Relief dropped him like a deadweight onto the bed. The last time he'd felt this giddy, he'd asked out his prom date. "Yes?" he echoed, needing to hear it again.

Laurence's smile was clear in his light laughter. "Yes, caveman. Something nice but not black tie, right?"

"No, not black tie, just not jeans."

"No *skinny* jeans?" Laurence teased with a throaty dare.

"Oh, God," he moaned. "Not fair." Josh stretched and fixed the swell of flesh beneath his zipper. That was when Josh realized he missed Laurence. They usually didn't see each other every day, and certainly didn't talk regularly, but now he would give anything to have Laurence there with him. Was it normal to miss him like this even though they'd just spent the entire weekend together? To crave his touch? His kiss? He could almost feel the decadent heat of roaming lips on skin. Josh wanted something other than a phone between them, like maybe just air. He knew that much, irrefutably.

"Hold on." The muted tap of the phone being set down was easy to hear.

Josh's eyes sank shut and he waited.

"Back."

"What did you do?"

"Saved my dinner."

Josh tossed his free arm over his eyes. "Oh, I didn't mean to keep you from eating."

"It's okay," Laurence murmured. "What are you wearing?" A throaty purr was in his voice and a complete surprise.

Josh burst out laughing. That unpredictability was one of the things he genuinely liked about Laurence. "I'm still dressed."

"That's a shame."

"What? Why?"

"Because I'm too far away to unwrap you."

Josh groaned. "Laurence."

"What?" he demurred with fake innocence.

Josh said the first thing to hit his tongue. "Wish you were here."

"Yeah?" A different kind of tension clenched his frame at that one breathed word. "Are you sure you want this, Josh? I... Well, I would understand if we stayed friends."

"Laurence." He growled, low in his throat.

"Yes?"

"Pack a bag and get over here." Laurence sucked a short gasp and moaned. Josh heard it all through the phone. The sounds he made sent shivers down his spine. "I haven't eaten yet. You can eat here."

"You want me to stay?"

Josh realized what he'd said, what Laurence was asking. "Come over, baby. We can have breakfast together."

Laurence definitely did whimper then.

LAURENCE KNOCKED once, the door popping open to reveal a smiling Josh on the phone.

"That's great, Professor Broker...Sean," he corrected after a short pause, a grin splitting his features. He winked and let Laurence shut the door. "Six-thirty? Yes, we'll both be there, and thank you again. Goodbye."

"First name basis?"

Josh shrugged, evading a little. "I've only met him once. He seemed nice." He replaced the phone on the counter, then he faced Laurence.

Laurence followed as Josh's gaze swept over him, top to bottom. Josh swallowed thickly. "Damn," he breathed.

"What?" Laurence dropped his bag, fearing a hole somewhere. He studied his front, twisting to see around his frame as much as he could, and found nothing. "Do I have a stain somewhere?" He'd changed from his earlier clothes, but he wasn't wearing slumming or slutty things either. He had no clue what had set off Josh like that.

"No, baby."

Laurence straightened, his breathing quickening beneath the simple endearment and sinful gaze locked on him.

Josh reached out and threaded his fingers into Laurence's hair. "You will tell me if I do something wrong?" he asked. "All I can think is how much I want to touch you, kiss you, and you look so damned good."

Laurence blinked, swaying into the strength of Josh's touch. A strength that was so gentle against him.

Something sizzled behind Josh, popping Laurence's eyes open. "Stove," he croaked.

"Oh, crap!" Josh jumped away and lifted the pan off the heat, giving it a shake. The smell of peppers and onions filled the kitchen, melded with an oregano sausage.

"That smells awesome." Laurence sidled up and peeked into the pan. Colors sizzled with the meat. A hint of garlic mixed with it all, rising on the waves of steam.

"I hope you like it."

"If it tastes like it smells, it beats the shit out of my scrambled eggs."

Josh laughed, turning off the burner. He plated it and carried both to the small table he had pushed against a wall. Laurence grabbed a couple cans of soda out of the fridge and sat with Josh at the table.

He moaned with the first bite. "Definitely. Eggs lose. This doesn't taste like store sausage."

"It's not. Mom sends it to me from the butcher back home. It's a private blend. She's been getting it since I was a kid."

"Really?" Laurence took another bite then wiped his mouth with a paper napkin. "That's sweet."

They ate in silence for a few minutes, the sound of forks scraping plates the only interruption. When Laurence was stuffed, he sat straight. "That was amazing."

Josh blushed, truly blushed. Laurence didn't think he'd ever seen the man do that.

"Want to watch a movie? TV for a while?"

"Sure." Laurence helped him clean up, getting the kitchen put back to rights in just a few minutes. If he happened to sneak a few touches of Josh's ass in his shorts, then even better.

Then they settled on the couch, Josh stretched out with his socked feet on the coffee table, and Laurence tucked into his side with one of Josh's arms over his frame, holding him close. He snuggled in, feeling relaxed and perfectly at ease. It was hard to remember RJ's cautions when he felt like this, content with a full stomach, warm against a hard body. Safe.

Now if that wasn't a shocker. Safe with Josh. He snorted.

Josh rolled on his neck, peering at him with lidded gray eyes. "Okay?"

"Perfect." He pressed into Josh's shoulder and he tightened the hold.

"Perfect. I like that."

Laurence smiled and sighed. Honestly, he did too.

The light stroke of Josh's thumb on his hip and the easy comfort of their breathing had his eyelids drooping. He knew he'd dozed off when the phone rang.

"Sorry, baby." He eased Laurence up with care, rather than dumping him off or jerking him out of his sleep. Once they were untangled, Josh stood and strode over to the phone. "Hello? Hi, Dad." He smiled and returned to the couch, urging Laurence down to use his thigh as a pillow. "No, it's going great. I don't know, Dad. I haven't really made up my mind about that."

Laurence listened with half an ear, Josh stroking over his arm, distracted.

"Well, I might be staying, anyway. The jobs are good and I have contacts. Gregory— You remember me telling you about him, right? —his are really starting to pay off." He made a noncommittal hummed sound to something his dad said on the other end. Laurence rolled to his back to stare up into Josh's face, watching his expressions as he answered a few more questions. The next thing was his eyes rolling. "Hi, Mom." Laurence giggled and Josh smiled.

Following on the heels of the caller changing to his mother, his face fell neutral and the stroking hand froze. "Mom. I appreciate it, but please don't. Tonya does not need my number. She was a friend in high school. I'm glad she's come home to help care for her dad, but she has nothing to do with me. Well, thanks for letting me know, but she is nothing but a friend, okay? Good." He sighed, his eyes closing, tension thickening his chest as he tried to breathe. "I'm working on it, Mom. Yes, seriously. Would this face lie to you?" His lips lifted into a quirked grin. There was a notable pause. "Actually, yes I do have someone in mind, but it's not up for discussion yet."

Laurence gulped. Josh looked right at him, then slowly relaxed, his touch resuming on Laurence's side as apparently the conversation switched topics again. Laurence tuned them out, wondering, replaying what Josh had said, guessing at his mother's side of things.

Oh shit. How is he going to tell them he's gay? Laurence's mouth went dry. First he doesn't want to take over the family ranch, now it's "Sorry Mom, I'm gay". Laurence cringed inside. Would Josh even do that? And as far as Laurence knew, Josh was an only child. It hadn't been cupcakes and rainbows when he'd come out to his own parents, though how they'd thought any different was beyond him. But Josh... Shit. The caveman. Gay. Laurence almost wept.

He was so fucked.

CHAPTER SEVENTEEN

JOSH LET OUT a sigh of relief when he finally hung up with his mother. He set the phone on the floor by the couch.

"Everything okay at home?"

Josh stroked a patient Laurence, gazing at him. "Yeah. Apparently one of my old high school friends was looking for me. I don't need my mother trying to find me a date," he joked.

"Tonya?"

"Yeah. We used to go horseback riding all over on the weekends. She's an awesome shot with a rifle." He did miss that, having the freedom to saddle up Buck and take off for a day. His old gelding was probably a rangy nightmare now, left out to pasture to be a free spirit.

"You are such a country boy."

Josh chuckled, running his fingers through Laurence's hair. "I know. I think I've adapted well. I can order a large coffee without needing a translator."

Laurence snickered, burrowing deeper against Josh's thigh. "You have come a long way," he agreed playfully. They watched a few minutes of TV in silence when Josh heard, "How do you think your parents are going to take..."

Josh glanced down and caught it when Laurence bit at his lip, not adding to it. "Take what?"

Laurence's eyes closed, though he was stiff beneath Josh's fingers. "Never mind."

"What, baby?" he asked gently. When Laurence wasn't forthcoming, he tapped him on the shoulder to get him to sit up. Once he was, Josh looped an arm around his waist and settled him comfortably on his lap. "You are so beautiful," Josh breathed, easing strands of blond away from his face. Blue eyes glistened with pleasure and he squirmed on Josh's thighs. "Now what about my parents?"

Laurence snaked his hands around Josh's neck and cuddled close. "How do you think they're going to take it that you're already dating someone?"

"They're going to be ecstatic," Josh replied.

"Even when you tell them I'm a guy?" Laurence fit himself into the crook of Josh's shoulder and neck, nuzzling skin to skin.

Josh let out a breath. *That* he wasn't too sure of. He hoped so. "What about your parents?" he asked. "You don't really talk about them."

Laurence shrugged. "What's to tell? Mom is a paralegal, Dad is an advertising exec. They have their own lives. Usually, he's on the road, or in the air."

"Do you talk to them?"

"Some."

Josh stroked up and down Laurence's back with a light hand. "How did they take you telling them you were gay?"

"They definitely weren't thrilled. My mom was shocked. Said she never saw it coming." Josh gave him a light squeeze when he snorted. "Seriously, that's only because she never paid any attention to those kinds of details. It wasn't like I hid things; I just wasn't outgoing about them."

"Out but not loud and proud?" Josh offered.

"Pretty much."

"Not to be mean, but there's no doubt now."

Laurence guffawed with a wicked tenor. "I'm more comfortable in who I am now."

Josh caressed the top of Laurence's head with a cheek, rubbing together while holding him close.

He wished he could imagine how his parents would take the news. He didn't think his parents would be against it, though shocked... That was likely a guarantee. Josh wasn't sure when he'd get the chance to tell them. He wasn't due for another trip home for a while with graduation looming. He hoped his parents would come for that, but he didn't want to ruin that accomplishment with this kind of announcement, and he had little doubt it would be shocking. He wondered if there ever was a best time for this type of news.

"You know, I'm going to screw this up, a lot," Josh warned.

Laurence leaned back to look him in the eye. The light rub of Laurence's thumb beneath one of his ears connected them more. "Just how serious are you about this, Josh?" When Josh scowled, Laurence rushed on. "I mean, do you think you'll be able to be out, eventually?"

Laurence's words slowed, and faded. Crystalline blue eyes searched, flicking from side to side, looking for something Josh couldn't name.

"I'm taking you to dinner on Thursday as my date, aren't I? I don't see Gregory or RJ being more than shocked, either. Anyone else?"

"So you're gay?"

Josh groaned in mild exasperation tempered with a smile and pulled him close again. Josh knew he wasn't a hundred percent ready to share this new side of himself with the world. For the moment, he was absolutely okay with Laurence in his arms, and just the two of them tucked away in private. *Baby steps.* Seemed to be the best plan of attack. "Shut up and watch the movie, Laurence."

Laurence hesitated then settled on his shoulder, clinging to Josh's body. Josh slumped a little, letting him curve against his frame easier. The slide also maneuvered Laurence's hip right over Josh's dick. Every few minutes, Laurence twitched, or adjusted and rubbed in hedonistic torture over his growing hard-on.

Josh knew it was going to take time to switch Laurence's view of him, maybe even more so than his own family. It had only been a few days, barely, since it had all come to a head after years of antagonism from both sides. One thing Josh did have was patience. He wasn't going to complain either that he had Laurence back in his apartment and in his arms. They hadn't gone so far as to have sex over the weekend, but there wasn't much more than that left unexplored between them. Josh was letting it build up. As much as he wanted to know all of Laurence, the wanting was driving him insane.

He dipped his head and pressed his lips to the skin of Laurence's neck. Laurence shivered in response. Josh loved the way he smelled. Something vanilla and a hint of coconut, tropical. He wound a tender hand beneath the loose front of Laurence's shirt, rubbing light circles over his abdomen. Laurence wiggled in reaction.

Josh raised from the silken heat of his neck and Laurence followed, soft lips parted invitingly, pressing his body into Josh's shoulder when he tilted his head upward.

"You're amazing," Josh breathed. He flicked the button on Laurence's jeans free. Laurence canted to an angle and whimpered, arching now in Josh's embrace. "So sexy." He'd never known a woman as sexy, even wanton, and able to embrace that without shame. Laurence was a passionate creature. Josh couldn't stop touching him. Rich, pale lashes fluttered to close his eyes. With the snap undone on Laurence's jeans, he eased the zipper down, spreading material. No underwear. Josh's desire spiked, his body growing heated. Laurence's erection waited for him, long and pulsing, a single bead of moisture already at the tip.

Without a hesitant bone in his body, he ran his thumb over skin to catch it, then brought the captured bead to his mouth for the first time. The flavor burst on his tongue. Tangy and cool, a little bitter. It still fired a shudder down his frame like nothing he'd ever known before. Fingers delved into Josh's hair, stroking him with insistent, driving passes. Palming the remote for the TV, Josh hit the power button by memory to toss it onto the coffee table. Holding Laurence close, he curled him into his chest and stood.

"Josh!" he squeaked, wide-eyed.

"Hold on, baby." He tucked Laurence closer with a hand beneath his crooked knees, enjoying the way arms and hands clung. "Trust me, not the first time I've done this."

"Oh?" Laurence was fighting hard not to giggle.

"You're talented, but not even you can get into bed when you're unconscious."

Laurence gaped at him. "You did that?"

Josh cleared the bedroom doorway and settled him easily onto the bed. "Of course. Told you I've had a lot of time to think about all of this." Hovering over him on his palms, he pressed a kiss to Laurence's lips. "You got to call the shots yesterday. Now, it's my turn."

Laurence moaned, and the sound shot through Josh to settle near his heart. He loved the sounds Laurence made, sweet and husky, raw and uninhibited. Holding Laurence steady, he helped ease his shirt over his head, baring the smooth expanse of skin beneath.

One thing he'd discovered in the last few days was he loved stroking over Laurence's skin. Smooth as molten silk beneath his fingertips. Laurence arched like a cat beneath his palms, bending and pleading with quiet whimpers. Gliding with a feather-light touch down his sides, he hooked Laurence's jeans in his fingers and tugged them south. Laurence kicked free to lay on his back, watching Josh through hooded eyes.

Josh took in his fill. Long legs, lean hips, wide shoulders, smooth arms and chest. Though Laurence was pale, he wasn't ghost white, and it was a contrast to his hair and eyes. Spread out on top of his bedspread, Laurence looked like a confection, all sweet powdered sugar and caramel.

Leaning close, he inched onto the bed, ghosting caresses and lips to a hip, skating up to his ribs. Flesh rippled as stuttered moans filled the room. Josh sighed when fingers gripped his hair, holding him. Laurence's hips bucked when he nipped at the hollow gently.

"Easy, baby," he crooned.

"Josh." Laurence panted.

Josh's heart thudded, pounding in erratic bursts. He brushed over hollows with his nose, enraptured by the ripples cascading down Laurence's chest. "Do I really make you feel like that?" he whispered.

Laurence sucked air, his fingers lightly clenched through Josh's hair, holding Josh to his mission. "Unbelievable. Driving me crazy," he gasped.

Josh tilted, running the rough of his cheek lightly over flesh and Laurence almost jumped off the bed.

"Josh!" he cried, a needy howl that melted Josh completely.

Slipping down the bed, he let out a slow breath over Laurence's groin. Laurence tossed on the bed, then widened his straddle, offering himself. Knowing what he wanted to do, knowing what Laurence wanted from what he'd already given Josh, he dipped and drew a breath. Heady and masculine, a sweet hint of the vanilla that had to be his soap and all Laurence.

"Oh... Oh, shit." Laurence mumbled, gripping at the bedding.

"Hang on, baby," he warned, then ran his tongue over one of the soft-skinned globes of his sac. A keening cry split the air and Josh jerked up. "Did I do it wrong?" He'd die before he'd hurt Laurence.

Gasping, gulping air, Laurence shook his head. "No...no. So damned good. More." He raised from the pillow and gazed at Josh with bright, begging eyes. "Please. More."

Josh wasn't going to wait for a second request. Licking his lips, he nuzzled down into the vee of Laurence's legs and lapped. Laurence's thighs trembled on either side of his head. Twirling his tongue, he teased and laved, played and suckled.

Laurence's leg twitched, and without breaking pace, Josh hooked both legs and drew them over his shoulders. Josh rose up to rest on his calves, lifting Laurence off the bed, all but immobilizing him.

"Josh! Shit, what... Oh, fuck, yes!" Laurence tossed, arching into Josh's mouth. Small heels pinned him, keeping him to his task.

Josh grasped his ass in his palms and held him still, then repaid some of the torture Laurence had dealt him over the weekend. One thing that was inarguable, Laurence was a hell of a teacher when it came to what felt good.

With the flat of his tongue, he swept over Laurence's opening.

Thinking he should be cringing, he repeated the oral caress effortlessly. Testing, he pressed at the wrinkled skin, trembling when he felt Laurence's reaction vibrate the bed and his hands. The full clench and release of muscle, the shudder of his weight.

"Josh!" he keened. "Gonna come. Can't... Fuck! Can't..." Words degenerated into a babbling mess.

Josh didn't stop, pressing and licking, panting through his own hungers. He wanted Laurence to come, wanted to feel the explosion. Through the weekend, Laurence had been the one to guide them, to show Josh what felt good and how to touch. Josh wanted to give that back to Laurence, make him float in the rush of euphoria. He didn't relent, pressing with his tongue, nipping with his teeth and making little stabbing thrusts that pierced the flexing opening with the lightest of force.

It must have worked, because Laurence cried out, stiffening, tugging with both hands on the bedding as his body twisted and snapped in Josh's hands. White streams striped his belly, falling to his chest where Josh held him over the bed. Gently, he lowered Laurence's body, his length flushed with pleasure. His chest rose and fell in gasping heaves as he came down from the rush of his orgasm.

Sucking air himself, Josh stood a moment later to find a towel in the bathroom. Tenderly, he cleaned Laurence's frame, watching shivers strike in his wake.

Once Laurence was cleaned, he stripped, dropping his clothing where he stood. When Laurence's focus fell to him following his every motion, Josh felt like the luckiest man. This incredible, giving man was his. No woman had ever looked at him with that heat and need; no woman had ever lost themselves so beautifully to his touch.

"I want you," Josh whispered, the merest apprehensive tremor in the words. He knew what he was saying, knew what he was asking. Knew there was no going back.

He didn't want to.

Laurence nodded. "Grab my bag in the living room."

Once he returned with the overnight satchel, Laurence opened it and pulled out a single tube.

"We need this, and the condoms."

Josh swallowed to hide his turmoil and found spares from the weekend in the drawer of his nightstand. "Do you always carry that?" he asked, sitting, facing him on the bed to stroke a thigh lightly.

"No," Laurence replied, copying the tender caresses on Josh's arm and shoulder. "Was hoping, but wasn't going to press for something you weren't ready for."

Josh lifted a hand and cupping Laurence's jaw, kissed him. "I'm ready," he breathed over Laurence's lips. "Want you so much."

Laurence shivered, gazing up at him through his lashes. "Want to feel you inside me. Need you." The growled words lit a fire deep inside Josh.

Josh claimed his lips, sweeping gently over their softness, the full shape and decadent heat drawing him deeper into the man beneath his touch. Laurence sighed, opening to Josh's lightest flicks of tongue, the gentleness a marked change from the passion they'd both just tasted. Josh moaned, deepening the pressure, the thrust of his tongue when he realized that for this, Laurence was letting him move at his own pace, at his own speed.

Kissing those lips Josh, could hardly think of anything else. Then the sweeping touch of fingertips on his inner thigh dragged a low moan from his throat. Laurence was lightly stroking skin, teasing with his fingers, to taunt and caress without finding more. It was driving Josh insane with desire.

Clasping Laurence's hand within his own, he cupped them both around his leaking shaft. A shudder rocked his whole body as heat and need washed over him.

"Love that," Laurence murmured, watching him through unblinking eyes. "You don't hide anything."

"You make me feel so good," he returned, fully meaning the compliment.

Laurence's smile turned sultry. "Come here." He shifted on the bed, making room for a naked Josh. Bringing the captured hand upward, he drizzled several drops on the tips of Josh's fingers. "Get me ready, caveman. Want to feel you everywhere."

Josh gulped.

Laurence smiled patiently. "You won't hurt me."

Tilting to meet his blue eyes, Josh stretched along Laurence's side. With his weight held up on an elbow, Josh slipped his slicked hand between Laurence's slack legs, watching and listening for the cues.

"That's it," Laurence purred. His eyes fluttered at contact, and Josh barely dared to breathe.

Josh rimmed Laurence's rosette, his heartbeat stuttering at the sensation of the muscle clenching again. He was beginning to think he really liked that reaction. Taking the next step, he glided a stiff finger through the muscle.

Laurence pursed his lips, sighing through an *ooo* as he tossed a little on the bed. Remarkably, just minutes since his last release, Laurence's dick began to twitch.

"Feels good?"

"Incredible," he managed. "Keep going. Another."

Taking his time, he learned what Laurence loved, stroking in and out, spreading his fingers apart to caress his inner walls, amazed and awestruck. The pressure on his fingers made him imagine how it would feel wrapped around his shaft, filling that silken heat as deep as he could go.

"Oh!" Laurence jumped and moaned a deep throaty sound.

"What?" Josh froze.

"Again. Prostate. Again!" he whimpered.

Carefully, Josh crooked his fingers and discovered the bump of nerves he must have hit.

Laurence growled and pushed down, impaling himself harder when he strummed skin.

"More?" Josh waited.

"Need you. Please, Josh." Laurence's dick twitched, full and stretching toward his navel again.

Leaving Laurence's heat, he quickly donned a condom, rolling it down his shaft. Focused as he was on Laurence, he'd been able to push his own needs out of reach, but the instant he held his own flesh, he ached like he hadn't had release in years.

Reaching for the lube, he dropped extra on his length, swirling his hand over the latex. "Ready, baby?"

"God, yes, please." He opened his eyes and pierced Josh with a sky blue so bright, he fell into them like spring pools.

Emotion swamped Josh. Shaking himself to concentrate enough to not hurt him, he slid between Laurence's straddled legs. And stopped.

Staring up his lean body, he said, "I don't want to hurt you." Josh was trying to figure out how he was supposed to fit. Josh wasn't huge, but the disparity still made him pause.

Laurence tugged a pillow from behind his head and managed to wiggle his little butt onto it without too much trouble. "Trust me, Josh. I want you, like this." He lifted a hand and caressed his bottom lip with a thumb. "Love me."

Josh couldn't fight that. Taking a slow, easy breath, he palmed Laurence's hips in gentle grasps, holding him to inch forward. He caught his lip to worry between his teeth when he sat nestled at the cusp.

The touch of a light hand brought his attention back to Laurence. The patience and wanting in his face was more than Josh could deny. His jaw fell open when he breached that pert ass, his eyes wide at the firm hold on his dick.

"Nice and slow," Laurence urged, a slight shudder rolling over his shoulders as pleasure darkened his cheeks.

Josh did, advancing to retreat, feeling the heat, the smooth silk of Laurence's channel as it gripped at him, held him prisoner, sucking him deeper with each thrust. He'd never experienced anything like it, like Laurence, in his lifetime.

He gazed into Laurence's eyes. A fresh tremor ripped over him as his eyes fell closed, swamped in the rush of emotion, his hips held frozen, Laurence's frame pinned by his.

Slowly, he began to move, gliding out to almost be free then in, filling Laurence's body, joining with him, becoming one in a way he'd never imagined. Lifting Laurence's feet to his chest, he thrust, watching the play of pleasure and desire flare wildly over Laurence's face. His eyes were shut tight, hands clawed deeply into the bedding as he rocked his hips in time to Josh's motions. Wave after wave of muscled heat gripped and stroked over Josh's cock. A slight change in pitch and Laurence bucked, gasping and mewling for more.

Josh knew what he'd hit and did it again. And again.

"Josh! So close!"

"Come for me, baby. Do it." Josh's voice was raw and growly from harsh breathing filling tortured lungs. The weight of his balls was tight, slapping against the smoothness of Laurence's ass, drawing closer with each hard piston of his body.

Laurence raised his hands and fisted his dick, whipping it with a wild pace, matching Josh's thrusts.

Bright passion burst a second before he stiffened under Josh, his head jammed into the pillow, his jaw locked tight. Streams of white pulsed from the swollen tip of his cock, coating his hands and his stomach in thick dollops.

Josh roared, thrusting deep, wanting to get as deep as he could into that silken heaven. Gliding in jerked passes, he jetted into the condom. The force of the orgasm left him boneless and he sagged onto his calves, limply holding Laurence in place.

Minutes or hours passed before he felt able to move. Backing away, he gently slid Laurence prone to the bed, his lover's breathing a panting echo in the room. Holding the condom as he slipped away from Laurence's glistening body, he stumbled from the bed for the bathroom to dispose of it and wash his hands. Grabbing a cloth and fresh towel, he wet the first and carried them both with him to the bed. Feeling a wash of tenderness he'd never experienced, he lovingly cleaned up the strength of Laurence's proof of his own release to toss both toward the hamper in the corner. Ditching the one pillow on the floor, he rolled Laurence beneath the sheets and pulled him into his chest. A kittenish nuzzle and sighing purr was all Laurence seemed to have the strength for.

They fell asleep between one slow, languid kiss and the next.

CHAPTER EIGHTEEN

"I WANT TO ring the doorbell!"

Josh chuckled at Laurence's playfulness but didn't restrain him when Laurence dashed up the last two steps to punch the button. Muted gongs echoed through the carved wood front door. Like he could deny Laurence anything. It had been hard to look away from Laurence's lean beauty when they'd been dressing. Black slacks which sculpted his waist and hips were complimented by an ice blue button down silk shirt. The man looked incredible. Josh had made himself walk out of the apartment rather than toss him over a shoulder and take him right back to bed.

Josh smiled when Sean opened the door for them. "So glad you could make it." He offered his hand to shake. Josh made the introductions between Sean and Laurence, shaking hands as well. "Come on in. A drink before dinner?"

"Sounds great." Josh followed, with a light hand on Laurence's back, keeping him close. Since Monday, they'd practically been inseparable. He wasn't complaining one bit, either.

Walking into a library with shelves upon shelves of books, Josh spotted Misha and

Natáli, sitting comfortably on a leather couch, talking quietly over wineglasses in their hands, but when they walked in, both stood.

Sean stopped next to the young pair. "Laurence, this is Misha and Natáli." They shook hands. Once the introductions were done, he walked a few paces to a drink bar and after dropping a couple ice cubes in each, poured from a crystal decanter into the three tumblers.

Natáli approached Josh to greet him with an outstretched hand. "Pleasure to see you again, Mr. Daily."

"Josh, please." Natáli's smile grew in wattage. Then Misha walked up behind Natáli and wrapped his arms around a trim waist. They were very similar in looks, and likely in age. Straight black hair, deep mysterious brown eyes, and features that were too pure, likely a mirage to hide a more devilish demeanor, one Josh felt their demurring attitudes likely hid. He'd seen the kind often in his classes. A pocket of trouble just waiting to happen. They reminded him of Laurence, and he knew his lover's wicked ways.

"I love your names," Laurence said, accepting a tumbler from Sean with a quiet thank you.

"We were both born in the Ukraine."

"Really?" Laurence asked, his curiosity rising.

Natáli nodded.

When Sean sat, both young men flanked him, curling to sit on their hips against Sean's sides, and Josh followed to an opposite facing couch, Laurence at his side. He caught a questioning glance out of the corner of his eye but then it was gone. Laurence hadn't paid them any attention at Club Six the previous weekend, so witnessing the three together was new to him.

"How did you meet, then?" Laurence asked, hooking a leg over a knee to sit forward. He sipped from his drink, palming it to listen.

Natáli giggled softly and rested on Sean's shoulder. "It is quite a story."

"There's time before dinner," Sean murmured, bringing him close to kiss the top of his head. Josh couldn't believe the show of affection, so open and unguarded. "I was doing research in Italy, and Misha and Natáli were traveling into Rome. You see, these two had developed a scheme. One would disarm and distract and the other would rob their mark blind."

"They robbed you?" Laurence gasped, whipping to take in the two placid expressions.

Sean urged the young pair closer. "They tried. But they had never met someone like me."

Misha settled a hand on Sean's thigh and after an acknowledgment, continued. "I have been best friends with Natáli since we were boys. We didn't realize growing up that wanting to be together made us different. When it was discovered, we were banished from our homes."

Laurence neared for comfort into Josh, and he wrapped an arm over his waist, holding him.

"We lived the only way we knew how then. Together, we could survive, but we had to go someplace where we could do that. Many in Rome like the young men." Misha pursed his lips in a twist of distaste. There was no missing the implication of how they had survived.

"How old are you?" Laurence asked, engrossed in the tale.

"I am twenty-four now, Natáli is eight months younger."

"When did you meet?" Josh was becoming swept up into their story as well. He left his free arm over Laurence's waist, companionable contact, and a small thrill shot through him when Laurence leaned closer.

"They were barely sixteen then, and on the run for more than three years. They were a pair, and a mess. They spoke broken English at best, because they'd lost their schooling. When they tried to steal my equipment, not even knowing then what it was, only that it had to be valuable, they met me."

Both younger men dropped their gazes then, deferring to Sean again the way they had in the club.

"I brought them home, got them back into school, and instructed them until they were eighteen, then they had a choice to make."

Josh squirmed a little, enthralled but worried hearing the rest may not be something he could understand.

"You were going to kick them out too?" Laurence gasped, appalled.

"Of course not," Misha chided with a smile. "Sean had opened his home to us, and his heart, but we didn't see it. We knew we were lucky. Lucky to have not been handed over to the authorities, lucky to still be alive, lucky to have found a giving man at all, but believing he could love us..." He glimpsed toward Natáli. "We have been all the other had known to that point. We didn't trust it."

"It was a hard time," Natáli added, an accent now more pronounced than Josh had noticed before. It could be why Misha did most of the talking.

Misha picked up the story again. "There was no promise, no requirement to pay him back for all he'd done. But, and this was the hardest of all. We could go if we wished. He held nothing over our heads, except we *couldn't* leave him. We physically could, but we would be missing a huge part of someone who had become such a large anchor in our lives. Realizing we loved him as much as we do each other was enlightening, but it didn't make everything happy then."

"No?" Laurence held himself up on cupped hands, elbows propped on his knee, listening avidly.

Sean threaded fingers through hair, caressing each young man in his palm. "I am a Dom. These young men are the light of my life, and mine. The choices they had to make were not for everyone, and I wouldn't have held it against either if they couldn't accept my terms. I would have been heartbroken, but I have already learned the hard way that trust and love must be part of any relationship. We all had to be willing to compromise."

"So...you're a Dom...and they're your...submissives?" Laurence asked on a respectful, awed note, sitting straight. When Misha and Natáli both nodded, Laurence asked in the same lowered tone, "Do you wear collars?"

In unison, they peered at Sean and giving them approval, both men sat up and lifted a pant leg apiece, exposing ankles. A thin, black ink tattoo of a wrapped cord was drawn, knotted and decorated with a dual pendant charm.

Misha pointed to the engraved charms on the cords, one a vibrant, almost blood red, the other rich, bright blue. "This one is Sean's, and this one is Natáli's. The day I made the decision was the hardest and best of my life." Natáli nodded in agreement. They dropped the hems of their pant legs and retook their positions. "We knew what Sean wanted and needed but had never so much as kissed before."

"The decision was theirs and I would not accept only one, because then they would not be complete themselves. It was a delicate situation."

"But you're so happy," Josh remarked.

Sean quirked an eyebrow, the side of his mouth mimicking it. "And you are not?"

Josh faced Laurence. "I am now." Laurence blushed, ducking his head.

"No war is fought and won with just one battle," Sean stated, taking a leisurely drink. Josh joined him, tasting his own scotch, letting the flavor roll over his tongue. He knew it was

Sean's way of advising him on how to win and keep Laurence. So far, he hadn't been wrong.

A chime sounded beyond the room. "Dinner is ready."

Unfolding from the couch, Laurence waited for Josh, then with a hand to Laurence's back, they followed Sean and the other two from the library.

"YOU DO REALIZE, we're not like that," Josh pointed out after the salad plates had been picked up. A lull had fallen between them and the lighter discussion they'd been sharing.

Laurence sat at his side, the table comfortable for the five of them, a round that likely could sit twelve but was set for just them. He wasn't sure who was minding the table and plates but Sean and the other two seemed oblivious to them. Maybe they were help for tonight. He knew Professor Broker was rich, but he'd never been in a situation with maids or butlers or help on hand. He just tried to use the right fork and not drool when the smells from the kitchen made his mouth water.

"I do, but I didn't invite you to try to convert you." Sean studied them with mild humor in his dark eyes. "I believe that we should have friends outside of our usual circles. I want Natáli and Misha to experience life, and have friends for themselves. Friends are just as important as loved ones in our lives. Don't you agree, Josh?"

Misha leaned toward Laurence. "He's usually not this uptight. He's trying to make a good impression. He likes you two."

Sean gurgled a laugh, and Josh covered his mouth with a napkin. Laurence smiled at his broad impertinence.

"It is true." Sean sighed with a wide grin. He relaxed into his chair. "Can't get anything past these two. They keep me on my toes."

"I know Misha is going to the university. Are you studying, Natáli?" Josh asked.

Natáli lifted his wine glass, drinking slowly, then setting it down. "I am. Anthropology."

"I love that!" Laurence beamed at him. "All the mysteries and legends, ancient worlds and societies."

"It's very exciting," Natáli replied with a shy voice. "I love the histories of the old tombs in Egypt, studying the different cultures."

Discussion flowed around the table. More about Sean's work, a story from Natáli about the catacombs of the ancient pharaohs. Even Misha's own studies, following in Sean's footsteps of Astrological physics. Laurence was circling the whole dynamic of Sean, Misha and Natáli. He knew a little about Dominant and submissive lifestyles, but had never known anyone who lived it. The last thing he'd expected was to find three people who were so comfortable with themselves, and the life they shared, and not just a couple, but a ménage.

Once all were done, Sean asked, "Join us on the patio for a few minutes, if you don't have to rush off."

Laurence peered up at Josh and smiled. He wasn't in a hurry.

"We'd love to," Josh replied for the both of them.

Sean stood from his seat. "Misha, please show them. I'll let Glenda know we're moving outside."

Misha looped an arm through one of Laurence's. "It's lovely outside. We usually sit out after dinner on the weekends."

With Misha guiding the way, they followed him through the house to a large, bricked patio with an expansive yard beyond it. Cushioned furniture was interspersed with tables and when Misha sat, he tugged Laurence down beside him. When he glanced up, Josh was grinning and winked at him, taking a solo chair a few inches away. What surprised Laurence was when Natáli sat on the ground next to a second couch. A moment later when Sean joined them, he curled around a leg and clung like a contented monkey. Sean threaded fingers through his hair, soothingly. Natáli's eyes fluttered and he almost preened into the caresses.

"I have to tell you Josh," Sean said. "You and Laurence are a striking couple. I'm glad you could both join us."

Misha still had his arm locked through Laurence's, his head resting on a shoulder in camaraderie.

"I worried you might have taken what happened at Club Six as intrusive."

"You were there?" Laurence asked as Josh waved away the concern.

"We all were," Misha replied. "It's his fault for finding two dance fiends." Misha sent Sean a teasing kiss through the air. Sean chuckled, without a worry.

"Oh, yes! I love to dance." Laurence wiggled on the cushion.

"You dance like a wild thing," Natáli purred, his eyes half closed. "I wish I had that kind of rhythm."

"Maybe you'd like to join us tomorrow, both of you?" Sean spoke to Josh. "They can dance and we can enjoy the show." Sean growled, getting giggles from the young men.

"Do you go often?" Josh asked.

"Usually once a month, but the boys have been studying hard for finals, so Friday nights I let them unwind."

"Please, Josh," Laurence asked before he realized it. It didn't even occur to him that he didn't *need* to ask, but he knew he wouldn't go without him, either. And if Misha and Natáli were as much fun as he sensed beneath their calm, he'd be dancing for hours. *And not have to worry about one hookup.* That right there was worth it to go with them. He certainly didn't want to have another "Ted" issue happen. He knew he wouldn't be looking for it. Aware how out of his comfort zone the dance club was, he waited for Josh to answer, though they were interrupted by a young lady carrying a tray of cups and a carafe of coffee.

"Thanks, love. See you in the morning."

Glenda smiled and tipped her head, then whirled to leave them.

"You have maids?" Laurence sat back and Misha lifted from where he held onto Laurence though he remained beside him. Laurence knew there'd been two servers at dinner, but Glenda wasn't dressed the same, more casual, and seemed more relaxed with Sean.

"She's our cook and is glad to help when we have company. I can't boil an egg and these two would live on french fries if I let them." More giggles shook the seat beneath Laurence.

"It's true," Misha whispered, his brown eyes dancing. "Love them."

"Please come," Natáli implored between Laurence and Josh.

Taking a filled bone china cup, Laurence studied Josh. "Are you up to going again?" he asked. Spotting the cloud that darkened his features, Laurence knew he was remembering last weekend as well. "I'll be with you, period. No one else."

Something hot and possessive gleamed in Josh's gray eyes at those words. "That goes without saying," he replied in a rumbled bass. A shiver shot down Laurence's spine. Josh relaxed into his chair, saying to Sean, "Count us in."

Laurence almost cheered, knowing what a large step Josh was making. Club Six was wild and now he'd be a part of it, not just watching from the sidelines. Laurence bounced a little, catching Misha's smiling attention. They shared a wicked grin then returned to the conversation and after dinner coffees.

CHAPTER NINETEEN

"ARE YOU ready yet?" Josh called into the bedroom. He checked his pockets, making sure he had what he needed, and still there was no Laurence. They were supposed to meet Sean and his boys in less than an hour, and Laurence had been stuck in the bathroom for the last fifteen minutes. Josh rolled his eyes when he heard footsteps. Laurence was such a peacock. Everything had to look just right. Not that he'd complain. The man was simply gorgeous.

Laurence hopped into view, shoving a foot into a sneaker. Then stopped cold, his foot falling with a carpet silenced slap. "Holy shit."

Josh froze. "Whaaat?" His eyes widened and he swallowed, ready for the worst. What did he do wrong?

"You are *hot!*" Unexpectedly, Laurence rushed him and jumped into his arms, linking his legs around his waist and clinging arms over his neck. "I'm going to go insane watching you all night in this T-shirt." Laurence ran a hand over the front of Josh's chest. "It's a good thing you don't wear stuff like this often. We'd never leave."

Pinning him close with his hands splayed across his spine, Josh buried his nose into the crook of his neck and shoulder, finding the sweet scent that he'd grown to adore about Laurence. The hickey was a fading memory, but he knew exactly what it had looked like. He swept his tongue over where the merest shade still bruised his skin. "You look good enough to eat." He nibbled gently and Laurence rolled his hips against him. "Love these damned jeans. Always have."

Laurence stretched out and gave him a dirtier than dirty grin. "I can tell." He purposely ground down and Josh shuddered.

"Behave."

"Not on your life," he retorted.

Josh laughed freely. "That's exactly what I'm scared of." After a quick, ferocious shared kiss, he set Laurence on his feet.

Before he could turn or move a foot, Laurence had hooked a belt loop of his jeans, halting him. "Josh? I know this is difficult, and I just want to tell you how happy I am that you're doing this, that you're trying. It's not easy to make changes like this, for anyone, no matter how long they've had to 'think on it'."

Josh cupped his face and stared into blue depths that owned him, heart and soul. "This has been the best week of my life, Laurence. I want to make those weeks into months, and maybe, just maybe, into years."

Laurence shivered, nuzzling into Josh's palms. "I really like how that sounds," he murmured, affection clear in every sound. It made Josh's heart pound with hope. Maybe he could do this.

"Have you thought about how you're going to tell your family?"

His high popped like an over-expanded balloon. His hands fell, limp. He wasn't sure how he was going to do it, and had no idea how they would take the news. He didn't believe they would treat him the way Misha's and Natáli's families had. There was no guarantee though. It would come as a total shock to them, and he knew it would hurt them. He hated the thought of that.

"No."

"Shit. I'm sorry." Laurence thudded his head into Josh's sternum. "Not pushing, I swear." He looked up and all Josh could find was sincere empathy. "Let's go have some fun, okay? Forget I opened my big mouth."

"Okay. Kiss me first," he said. Laurence wrapped his arms around Josh's neck and reached for all he was worth, stretching upward. Josh tingled from his nape to his toes by the time Laurence let him stand straight.

When they arrived at the club, a line was already nearly to the corner as they drove by to find a place to park. "Damn. Guess we'll have to wait." Laurence didn't look too thrilled either. He'd been bouncing in his seat the entire drive from the apartment.

Reaching the line to wait their turn, Josh kept Laurence close. The man knew how to dress to tease. He was wearing skin tight "lick this" jeans and a skimpy, paper-thin A-shirt in silvery gray. The color did amazing things for his eyes. It showed off everything from shoulders to fingertips, and hid nothing beneath it. He beat Josh's black T-shirt by miles, but he was stretching to wear what he was. Josh didn't usually wear things with sex on the brain, but he'd do whatever it took to make Laurence happy. Knowing Laurence couldn't keep his hands off Josh more than made up for any discomfort.

"Hey, Josh." A hand clapped him on the shoulder.

He spun, guarding Laurence easily behind his frame.

"Chill. Lingo, remember?" He dropped his hand to shake. "Come on. Sean and the boys are already inside. You're on the guest list." He started to walk away, and Josh caught Laurence's confused gaze. Before they lost Lingo completely, they slipped past the milling crowd in line to the front door.

Lingo leaned in and spoke to the doorman. "Bill, they're on the guest list under Sean Broker."

"Not a problem. Have fun." He unlatched the velvet rope that last weekend they'd waited to get through and followed Sean's driver into the club.

"Seriously? *A guest list*?" Laurence asked, though it was an attempted whisper considering the noise level.

Josh rolled a shoulder. He had no clue.

When they approached the gathered group, Misha jumped up from his seat beside Sean and hugged Laurence, Natáli right behind him, though not trying to knock him off his feet with his own exuberant greeting. Sean shook Josh's hand.

"Glad to see you, and might I say, you both look delicious," he drawled with a teasing leer.

Josh blushed while Laurence gave him a cheeky wink. Drinks were ordered and conversation was soon zooming between Laurence, Misha and Natáli. Lingo stood to the side, tapping out a rhythm to the music, one eye on the group and one eye everywhere else.

"I'm glad to see that," Sean murmured. "They've been through so much. I protect them, but I don't want them sheltered."

"Hopefully this isn't too inconsiderate, but how much older are you?" Josh rested an arm on the bench behind him, sitting next to Sean while the wild three chattered and laughed themselves into fits.

Sean met his gaze out of the corner of his eye. "I'm thirty-six. I was in my twenties when we collided." A look that was filled with love no one could question fell on both of the dark heads at the table. "I knew I wanted them, loved them, but they were so young. It was agony letting them grow up. I wasn't always the nicest guardian," Sean admitted. "But I always tried to be fair." Touching shoulder to shoulder, he added, "And before you think it, I didn't touch a hair on either of them until they were well over eighteen and both knew what they were getting into."

"The tattoos? When did that happen?" Josh leaned forward on his elbows to be able to hear better.

"Only two years ago." A memory Josh couldn't even guess at lightened his expression. "They came to me, unified and committed. I actually refused them the first time. They convinced me that I was the one being foolish then. I've never been happier." Sean sipped at his drink, a cocktail in a highball glass. "How are you and Mr. Gorgeous doing?"

Josh coughed into his beer, feeling the flushed heat fill his face again. "Please, his ego is bad enough." They both laughed. "I'm here, and he was my date last night. Every day is easier."

"But..." Sean encouraged.

"This is segregated," Josh conceded after a pregnant pause. He was cocooned from real life in the club, at his apartment, at Sean's. He wasn't going to hide from that fact. He knew he wasn't really ready to face the outside world as a gay man. Every argument and dissection between himself and his conscience replayed on a loop.

Josh's gaze flowed over bobbing heads, other couples already together, and those doing like himself, just talking and people watching from the tables surrounding the madness of the dance floor. "None of our closest friends know yet, or my family." Thinking about what Laurence had asked twice already, he knew he wasn't looking forward to breaking that news.

"It is what it is," Sean remarked. "Those that love you, will. Who you are with will not change that. For those who can't accept, then they cannot accept anyone's evolution. No human stays stagnant. Life ensures that, Mr. Daily." He tapped his glass to Josh's bottle and drew a sip.

"Why did you really invite us? Me?"

Sean didn't seem at all put off by the directness of the question. "Honestly, because

I do like you, and something on your face last weekend struck me. I knew that feeling, that pain. I know nothing is guaranteed other than death once we are born. We must make life happen. I stopped making apologies a long time ago."

"Master?"

Sean lifted his head. Three hooligans stood before them. "Yes, Misha?"

"May we dance? With Laurence?"

"Keep your clothes on," he warned them in an indulgent tone of someone who knew what the odds were. He offered a hand and both came forward and kissed him gently, cementing their commitment further.

Not to be outdone, Laurence circled the table and ran a seductive hand up Josh's thigh.

With a firm grip on a jean clad hip, Josh brought Laurence into the gap of his legs. "I second that, glow stick. Keep your clothes on. You're too gorgeous to be seen naked in this crowd."

"Gonna make me?" Laurence teased with a saucy tilt to his head.

Josh nipped at an earlobe, chuckling. "Like I could," he whispered just for Laurence. "One of the things I've always loved is your wildness."

Big and blue, his eyes shot wide, to blink in surprise.

"Go have some fun. I know what dancing does for you."

That got a lengthy, throaty purr from Laurence. "Only for you now."

"God, you're making me hot. Go!" Josh kissed him hard then gave him a gentle push, and like a shot, all three ran for the dance floor, hand in hand.

"He's as much a menace as my boys."

"Utterly," Josh agreed, too content to care.

The music vibrated the air and the three of them undulated like wild creatures, arms in the air, hips gyrating. Josh swallowed some of his beer instead of his tongue. This was a sight he'd mostly missed last Friday, Laurence becoming one with the pounding beat. It wasn't helping that he had two more just like him, darker, playful, and vibrant egging him on. Laurence ate it up. The three were oblivious to the lusting gazes following their every move from every corner of the packed hot spot.

"Oh shit," Josh hissed. They'd made a Laurence sandwich, bumping and grinding and doing as lewd a dance as they legally could with their clothes still on. He dropped a hand under the table to adjust his aching shaft in his very tight jeans. It didn't help.

"I have to agree." Sean took a large swallow of his drink, just as engrossed in the decadence of their movements. "That is stunning."

Josh didn't know when his beer dried up or when a fresh drink appeared, but he sucked it down, trying to cool the fire in his belly from watching the three men. Arms swung above their heads, hands linking and pulling, guiding as they rocked their bodies in a single motion, sex personified. Misha released hands to wrap one around Laurence's waist, reaching for Natáli in the front.

Josh couldn't tear his gaze from the sheer rapture on their faces. A small circle had widened around the three of them, and still they danced, oblivious to everything around them. Then almost in silent unity, they pulled apart and captured Natáli between them, grinding against hips and thighs as they clung to shoulders. Sweat made all three glisten, the strobing lights sparking off them as though they were electric themselves. Josh wanted to lick it off, wanted to feel the race of blood as it pulsed through Laurence's body.

Thankfully for his sanity, the music changed and in agreement, holding hands, they returned for a well earned break. Several nearby applauded them as the two took their places flanking Sean. Laurence didn't sit, instead strutting right up to Josh and climbing onto his lap.

"Helllooo, Santa," he crooned, digging hungry fingers into Josh's hair.

"You've been a very bad boy," Josh replied, playing along. "Santa doesn't give toys to bad boys."

"Yeah, but I bet I can get Santa to change his mind," he challenged right back.

Josh threw his head and laughed, deep and loud. "I have no doubt." He wrapped his arms around Laurence's lithe frame, curling him into his body. Unable to resist, he swept his tongue up the column of Laurence's throat, groaning as the flavor of Laurence's skin burst in his mouth. "So damned sexy," he murmured against flushed skin.

After a few drinks and a chance to catch their breaths, Natáli shouted across the table. "Ready for more?"

"Hell yeah!" Laurence whooped. He twisted on Josh's lap, a splayed hand on Josh's chest. The single touch scorched him. "Come out soon?"

"I can't dance."

"No one here can, but we fake it really well," he offered with one of his cheeky smiles. After watching them on the dance floor for the last hour, Josh would have to disagree. Laurence was as graceful as any trained dancer.

Seeing what Sean was up to, he caught them in a three-way kiss-fest. Josh swallowed hard. He was practically in overload as it was, and then *that*. He groaned, pressing his forehead to Laurence's shoulder, stealing another peek. If they had no shame to do it so openly, then Josh wasn't going to turn away. His dick pulsed again, confined in agony and he moaned.

"They're dangerous, aren't they?" Laurence asked close to Josh's ear. The brush of his lips tickled the shell of Josh's ear.

"Sex on legs," Josh agreed. He had no idea how Lingo survived them. He seemed way too unaffected by it all. Maybe he was a eunuch.

Hopping off Josh's lap, Laurence grabbed his latest drink and gulped it. "Let's go guys!" he called when they'd stopped for air from Sean's kisses. They whirled and followed him once more out to the dance floor.

Josh sipped at his drink, not paying the least attention when a new one replaced the old. Anything to wet his parched mouth. He wasn't even doing anything, and he was practically panting.

"You weren't kidding about the show," Josh murmured close to Sean's shoulder.

"They can be a handful at times," Sean replied slowly, having as hard a time as Josh in tearing himself away from the three of them doing everything but having sex right there on the dance floor.

"Laurence knows what's too much." At least, he hoped so. The way they moved together was poetry. Laurence probably knew him better than he knew himself and would do nothing to hurt him, or their budding relationship. The fact that he trusted Laurence so deeply didn't faze him in the least. After four years, Josh completely trusted Laurence. He couldn't stop from watching them dance any more than Sean could. The sexual energy was so strong, he felt it on his skin, like it was a living, breathing force around them.

Not too much later, he got to feel that sensual pull up close and personal. In unison, all three stalked Sean and Josh at the table and refused to take no for an answer. Smiling indulgently, Josh allowed them to drag him to the dance floor. He had no idea what to do, but Laurence did and that was all that mattered to him.

CHAPTER TWENTY

JOSH HAD barely opened the door to his apartment before Laurence was climbing him. "Oh, God." His breath left him in a graveled moan. Laurence clung, his legs wrapped tightly around Josh's waist. Holding him close, he spun and braced Laurence against the wall, devouring his succulent mouth. Laurence was practically vibrating with need, sharp, keening whimpers slipping from his lips. With blind attempts, Josh managed to find and turn the locks, then sank to his knees right there in front of the door.

"Laurence. Can't stop touching you."

"Anything," he whined, undulating and clawing into Josh. "Drove me crazy tonight."

Josh had never seen anything as sexy as Laurence dancing. He'd had a hard-on since the first five minutes of watching Laurence with Misha and Natáli, and he didn't get thirty seconds relief all night. It hadn't helped one iota that Laurence had teased, rubbed and in general given him hell the whole ride home from Club Six. That place was an erotic haven. The energy. The sexy men. The way it turned Laurence on. And Josh got to reap the rewards.

"You were so bad," he growled. "Toying with your cock while I drove." A fierce shiver hit Josh. He could easily remember the sight of Laurence's hand stroking his dick, his jeans lowered to his ass to rub between his thighs and tease his balls. It was a wonder they hadn't wrecked. Or a testament to Josh's driving skills.

"Need you to fuck me, Josh." Laurence was begging, rubbing all over Josh like a lean cat.

Josh loved how Laurence's skin warmed to a rosy pink when he was aroused, when he caressed against the hair on Josh's arms and chest. And the squeals and purrs that came from his lover when Josh tortured him with his beard. There had never been anyone as perfect as Laurence for him.

A short pause in his attack came on the heels of a single thought.

I'm falling for him. Oh, shit. I'm falling for a man. Staring down into Laurence's crystal blue eyes, all he found was a hungry shimmer, an open need for Josh deep in their depths. Eyes that right at the moment were blown wide with a desire that only appeared for Josh. He couldn't label the emotion that one look brought to him. It was happiness and bliss and humbleness that Laurence wanted him so openly, hungered for him.

Braced over those lips, now puffy and red from their wild kisses, he gathered him in his arms. "Not making love to you on the floor," he growled.

Laurence blinked trying to focus, his hands digging into hair to massage Josh's scalp. Josh stood, tenderly holding him. Carrying him effortlessly to the bedroom, he gave Laurence an evil grin, then tossed him to the bed, where he landed with a bounce to explode into rolling laughter.

Josh ripped his T-shirt over his head, tossing it out of the way. "I'm going to lick every inch of your body," he stated, stalking up on the bed with a lumbering agility.

"Ooh! Yes! Tongue whip me, sexy," Laurence crowed.

Grasping at Josh's shoulders, Laurence tugged until Josh came down on top of him. Laurence's hands stroked him, his shoulders, his arms, his sides, anywhere he could reach, and each caress felt like a brand to Josh's skin.

Working Laurence's shirt up his frame, he tugged it over his head. "Leave your arms," he ordered. Laurence stretched them above his head, tightening his body. There was something about all that skin, the musk of sweat and the smoothness of his angles that scrambled Josh's mind. The shirt in his fingers floated over the side of the bed. In almost no time, he'd shimmied down Laurence's frame, loosening jeans to drag them down his body. Standing at the end of the bed at his feet, Josh ripped shoes off his feet, then with hard tugs, yanked socks and denim off, leaving Laurence completely naked on his bed.

"God, you're beautiful," Josh moaned. Laurence released a tremulous breath, his eyes sky-blue, bright and pinned on Josh where he stood over Laurence.

Leaning forward, he caressed long legs with his palms, trailing after with languid licks of his tongue. Laurence's gasp of shock said it all. Lifting his gaze to search up his body,

Laurence's cock bobbed, pulsing with need, a bright pink as blood filled him. There was something purely animalistic about Laurence, fully wanton that drove Josh insane for him. Soft, fine hair tickled his lips as he made lingering passes.

Placing seeking hands on ankles, he spread Laurence on the blankets. A faint whimper of excitement filled the room. Shivers of lust burned Josh's skin. He realized Laurence liked a little control. He noted his hands hadn't moved one inch since telling him to leave them above his head. Josh trailed light fingertips down the inside of his knee, kisses following and Laurence hissed. In short passes, he brushed flesh with the stubble on his cheek, hearing Laurence's reaction in his gasped bursts and throaty moans. The raw, needy rumbles were music to Josh.

Rising upward, he dropped hot, open-mouthed, sucking kisses to inner thighs, feeling the excited quiver beneath his lips. Drawing a breath, absorbing the scent that was all Laurence, he sucked at the softest skin at the edge of his groin and hip, tossing an arm over his waist to hold him immobile. A garbled shriek faded into stuttered gasps of air.

"Shit, Josh," he mumbled. He rocked restlessly on the bed. "So good."

A moment later, he eased up onto his knees. Laurence's chest was a rosy red, stuttering with each breath. The beat of his heart was a faint pounding against his ribs and skin. His lips were gently parted as he fought for air.

Reaching, Josh dug into the drawer and found the condoms. He shook a little as he opened it, and very carefully rolled it down Laurence's seeping length.

Laurence's eyes popped open. He bit on his lower lip, wanting in his eyes, but hesitant to say a word.

"Let me." Josh rubbed a gentle hand over his abdomen. A small release of emotion slid from him when Laurence nodded. Getting comfortable, he settled between Laurence's trembling legs. He massaged his balls, rolling them in a palm. It was heaven watching Laurence come undone. Josh let him go, giving him almost no time to catch his breath when he raised up on his elbows.

The latex was beyond unpalatable when he wrapped his lips around the crown. He jerked away.

"You don't have to, Josh," Laurence said.

He shook his head. "Just didn't think it tasted that bad. You make it look easy."

Laurence chuckled shakily. "I've done nothing else," he said. "If they refused, they didn't get me."

Josh scowled, not wanting to be reminded there had been that many before him.

"Caveman? Look at me."

Josh did.

"You're not a virgin, but we're together. That's what is important."

Josh whooshed out a breath. He nuzzled in close. "I know." He drew a breath. "Let me try again."

Laurence canted a knee and caressed his ribs. "It changes nothing if you can't."

Stunned silent, that was when he fell for him.

Bowing his head to hide from Laurence's knowing eyes, he tried again, this time aware of the spoiled sourness. Instead he focused on the heat, the hardness, as he took Laurence's dick between his lips for the first time.

He'd done plenty with women and knew his own body. None of it prepared him for the uniqueness of having his mouth filled with throbbing flesh. He moaned and Laurence hissed, a slight hitch of his hips impossible to miss. Something snapped, or connected. It was awkward, yet it felt perfect. It was male and it turned him on like nothing in his life. Careful of where he was, he sank all the way to the root.

"Fuck! Josh!" Laurence wailed, jerking on the bed.

Recognizing his reactions for pleasure, he rode him, twisting his mouth as he swirled around him with his tongue.

Laurence cried out, needy hungry sounds.

Josh wondered if he could make him come by sucking him off. On his knees, he braced his hands on either side of his hips and sucked, riding him. Laurence had done this a few times already, and Josh wasn't uneducated. Using what he knew he liked, he raked his tongue up and down his length, over the head, pressing down flat against him.

Laurence began to come unhinged. He thrust, little jerked pops that were punctuated by growing whimpered cries.

"Ah! Josh, yes." His head tossed on the pillow. "Yes! All of it!" He sobbed.

Josh tilted and rubbed the roof of his mouth over the tip. Laurence lost it. Arching, he shouted. An instant later, the throb of hardness beneath his lips changed, pulsed and Josh felt the heat of his release fill the condom.

Looking from beneath his lashes Laurence lay splayed, panting, melted. He released Laurence carefully unable to stop all of his smiling.

Standing on unsteady feet, he went to the bathroom and yanked a towel off the rod to return to the bedside. He tenderly unsheathed Laurence, wiping him clean to drop a final caring kiss on his skin.

The scent of his orgasm was musky and raw, only lightly tainted by the latex, but Josh knew he wanted that for the rest of his life. Melting Laurence.

Laurence's arms flexed. He'd hadn't moved them at all. Slowly, he unclenched his hands from the top of the mattress, licking dry lips. "Oh, God." He moaned.

"Good for a first one?" Josh asked, tenderly licking over a nipple and feeling the collection of shivers as they chased each other over smooth skin.

"Unbelievable," Laurence rasped, dry.

Once Laurence was cleaned, Josh removed his jeans and socks, shimmying out of his garments. He noticed the pile of packets on the stand was dwindling. He'd have to make tonight count.

Gazing down into the flushed face on the bed, Josh's heart pounded. He never saw this coming, and had run hard but in the end Laurence caught him. He hoped he could be what Laurence needed in return. He hoped Laurence could love him back.

CHAPTER TWENTY-ONE

LAURENCE'S BREATHING finally evened enough to be able to hear more than the erratic tide of blood against his ears. His lungs stopped heaving. It didn't help much. He still felt like he was on fire from the inside out. His eyelids weighed a ton as he fought to open his eyes and focus. The sight that greeted him made him crave.

Josh stood at the side of the bed, utterly, completely naked. Gray eyes flashed from below lowered lashes with a burning need and heat that bit hard at Laurence's own desires, stoking them anew. God, he was already growing hard again. No one had ever made him react the way Josh could.

"Can I move yet?" He bowed his spine in a fresh stretch, catching the way Josh zeroed in on his every motion. And loving it. There was no doubt he was Josh's total focus.

Josh chuckled. "I think you're going to need to."

"Oh?" Laurence purred.

Josh climbed onto the bed and stretched out at his side. "I'm going to make you scream," he warned with an evil glimmer in his eyes.

"Sexy, you already did," Laurence pointed out, smiling and unable to stop. He'd enjoyed every second of it, too.

"Let's see if I can make you do it again," Josh challenged, nearing to lick over Laurence's lips like he was candy.

Laurence moaned, a sighed murmur of sound. Driving demanding fingers into thick hair, he held Josh close when he started using that talented mouth again. Whimpers were constant as Josh stroked him, from shoulder to hip. He paused to flick and play with a tight nipple, rolling it between two not quite gentle fingers, then running in maddening circles around the smooth skin. Josh was in constant motion, his hands, his lips. He held to his promise, licking and stroking as much of Laurence as he could, up his throat, across his collar bones. Then he lowered and bit at his chest, little teasing plucks of skin between teeth.

Laurence jumped like he'd been electrocuted.

"Does my baby like that?" Josh throatily husked against flesh.

Laurence couldn't form words much less total sentences. Instead, he held him firm, encouraging more. He got it. Air hissed between his teeth as wild pleasure erupted. Even as he hungered for more, nothing he did made Josh move any faster, brought him any closer to fucking Laurence like he desperately needed.

Tenderly, Josh slid a hand between Laurence's thighs and rolled his sac, playing lightly with the small rounds of flesh. Shocks as huge as lightning bolts careened up his spine. His mouth fell open, and his neck arched as he cried out.

"Love that," Josh breathed, sucking on flesh and nerves until Laurence was trembling beneath him. "So wild, so beautiful."

No one... *No one* had ever manipulated Laurence's senses the way Josh was doing. When there was a press of entry at his ass, he quivered in need and widened his stretch as far as he could.

"Never been a slut, huh?" Josh teased him.

Laurence tried to blink, and managed to roll his head. "I didn't...wasn't... Oh, fuck." Laurence groaned long and loud, a thick finger filling him with one swift push.

"My little slut," Josh told him. "So pretty, wild. I want you to scream for me."

The torturous growl of Josh's words were stronger than any liquor they'd consumed that night. They went right to his head.

A new hickey was being raised on his chest. Laurence didn't care. He didn't care if Josh marked him all over. He was so hard again, he throbbed. His body was on fire. Then another finger joined the first and any instructing Josh may have needed had been well learned. Canted twists and scissoring motions were evil incarnate as he brought Laurence to a whole new plane of need.

Laurence tried to ride them, to impale himself on the filling sensation. Josh rolled his wrist, corkscrewing Laurence when he did.

Laurence babbled, crying for more, clutching at Josh and at the bed.

When Josh slid free, he tried to catch his breath. It rushed from him in an explosion as the full feeling returned.

"Shit, that is incredible," Josh whispered in awe. "So hot."

With the wiggle of his fingers, Laurence felt as he spread three of them. "Please, Josh. Fuck me fuck me fuck me fuck me..."

Instantly the fullness was gone and he cried in denial.

"Shh, baby." The bed moved and the sound of a condom opening gave him a moment's reprieve along with a velvet caress of electricity up his spine.

Josh repositioned himself. "Turn over, Laurence. Next time, I promise. Got to have you hard right now."

Laurence whimpered on the edge of his hunger. He managed to roll over and present himself. With Josh's careful hands cradling his hips, he pulled them together and entered in one full thrust. Laurence buried his face into the bed to stifle the scream, wiggling for more.

Either Josh understood, or realized he hadn't hurt him because there wasn't a moment's hesitation before he began pounding into him.

Lights sparked and scattered like fireworks on his closed eyelids with each driving thrust. His body wasn't his own. In that moment, he knew Josh owned him. Claimed him in a way no one in his lifetime ever had.

Fingers clawed into the bedding as he met Josh's snapped hip thrusts. The reality was beyond anything he'd dreamed in his imagination. Josh was perfect.

Shocks made him pant as their bodies came together. His world shrank to just the two of them and the intense sensation of Josh's cock striking inside and rubbing against him. So deep, Laurence was positive he felt him in his throat. And he loved it.

"More, sexy. Harder," he croaked.

"Oh, fuck." Josh's fingers dug in. "Hang on."

Laurence did.

He screamed when Josh let himself go. Laurence shook his head like a dog, bouncing jaggedly on the bed to feel everything, to feel every inch. Tingles of warning were growing, slicing up his spine. Tight twists shot blasts of need and desire from his nuts upward.

He went limp when strong arms banded his middle and hauled him up to Josh's lap. "Give me this, baby. Come for me," Josh growled. Then he began to jack Laurence off. Josh propped him on steady thighs, still impaled, and fucked him while he stroked his cock. "Mine," Josh breathed against Laurence's shoulder. Teeth and lips razed flesh then hung on, sucking and biting his neck behind his shoulder.

Laurence arched and stiffened, his balls tightening to shoot. "*Arrrh!*" Streams erupted like a geyser, spilling over Josh's hand and onto the bed. Josh moaned, graveled and raw. Bouncing Laurence twice, the clench of his ass, the heat of his orgasm set off Josh. With hoarse grunts, he ejaculated into the condom. The swirl of Josh's tongue over his latest brand stroked in tandem to Laurence's release, the clench and release of his seed as his balls wrenched out every drop to coat Josh's hand.

His next conscious thought was disorientated. He hung suspended from Josh's hold, still filled with the slick wet of the condom, which was very slowly shrinking. Josh was heaving for air.

Tenderly, he brought Laurence up by the chin and found him, lip to lip, nibbling softly. "Amazing, baby. Always be mine." He nuzzled close and managed one more sloppy, heartfelt kiss before taking them both to the bed at the side of their created mess. "Drive me insane, baby. The sounds you make."

Laurence tried to stroke him, an arm, a hand, and was too drained to make it. Josh's chest rocked as he laughed hoarsely. "Let me get us cleaned up." Inching away, Laurence felt impelled to follow that intense heat and fullness. Josh kissed his neck, his moist breath bathing him. "In a little bit, sweetheart. I promised to lick you all over. I'm only half done."

Laurence shivered, a moan breaking free before he could catch it. The bed sank when Josh rose.

When Josh woke him a few hours later, it was with the evil damp press of his tongue lapping over Laurence's hip and ass. They'd cleaned up as much as they could, stripping the blanket to toss to the floor before they'd curled up together to pass out.

Apparently Laurence's reprieve was over.

And he was loving every minute of it.

CHAPTER TWENTY-TWO

LAURENCE SMILED and waved as Roni left him in the library, his last tutor student for Monday. He let out a breath, closing the book and stacking his things to stash in his backpack. Mondays were always the hardest, especially after a weekend like the one he'd just had. Friday night dancing until the club shut down. In bed with Josh until noon on Saturday, and not just because they were wiped from dancing all night. Two weekends in a row. How many did it take to make a habit? He wanted this kind of habit. He bit his lip to not giggle.

He couldn't think of when he'd been this happy.

"I can't believe it." A shocked voice broke him out of his reverie.

"What?"

RJ sat across from him. "Is it true?"

"Again, I ask what?" Laurence had a feeling he knew what was coming, but didn't want to be the one to let Josh's secret out of the bag. He also decided he was going to have to change his tutor locations if RJ could find him so easily.

RJ pulled out his cell phone and showed Laurence a picture. Laurence blushed. *Yeah, can't argue that.* He was practically climbing Mount Josh for a kiss during one of their drink timeouts. Josh's hands weren't exactly innocent in the picture either. Damn, he looked hot in that T-shirt. A neutral expression slid over Laurence's features. He'd tried to convince RJ once already, without success. "And? Your point is?"

"He's really gay?" RJ seemed absolutely stumped. He looked at the picture then blanked the screen.

"How'd you get that?"

"The guy I met last weekend sent it to me. Wanted to know where I was since you two were there. And when I asked him *which* two, he sent me that, to my utter shock. You didn't answer your phone all weekend," RJ reproached.

Laurence dropped his gaze to the table between them. "I wasn't at my place."

"Josh's? *Again?*"

He winced at the quiet strident note. "What's wrong with Josh?"

RJ raked a hand down his face. "Laurence. He's going to hurt you."

Laurence pursed his lips. "I shouldn't be the one to say anything. It's his choice to tell anyone."

"Because he's not gay," RJ almost growled.

"Because he is," Laurence hissed right back, then paled. "Shit." He felt ill to his stomach, but he couldn't refute the picture. After bringing it up before their date on Friday, Josh hadn't mentioned coming out again, and honestly, it wasn't Laurence's decision or right to say a single syllable about it to anyone. Now there wasn't much of a chance of it not being known all over already. Especially if anyone from the university recognized him Friday. Gossip spread like wildfire in dry grass over the campus. "How many people saw that?"

"Just me, I guess." RJ shrugged.

Laurence's heart slowed. Some of the queasiness abated. "Look, leave it alone." He gripped the shoulder strap of his pack and hauled it up, settling the weight. "I can take care of myself." RJ stood too and joined him at the edge of the table.

"I know you can, Laurence, but I also know Josh."

Laurence shook his head. "You don't," he interjected gently. "You missed a lot this year, and it's the biggest thing I regret about you not being here, to share it."

RJ stuffed his hands into his pockets. "So, you're serious?" They started walking out of the library.

Was he? How serious was *serious*? "I'll let you know," he hedged.

RJ rolled his eyes but nicely opened the door anyway, allowing Laurence to go first. "I have some news."

"Yeah?" *Thank you. Topic change.*

"I'm getting an office. It's small and really only a sublet from another private business, but it's enough for me for now."

"That's great!" He watched where he was walking as he took the steps down. "Does that mean you're hiring someone?"

"I am."

"Woot! Mr. Entrepreneur!"

RJ chuckled quietly. "It's a start."

"Let's go grab something to drink. I have over an hour until my next course, then I'm done for the day."

RJ looked at his phone for the time. "I can kill most of that with you."

"You're on."

"HI, BABY," Josh said when he opened the door Monday evening. Laurence walked in, tossed his pack and launched himself at Josh.

He dropped a flurry of kisses over Josh's face. Josh spun and pinned him against the wall, managing to close the door with his arms full of clinging boyfriend. A rumbled moan slipped from him when he conquered Laurence's lips. "Miss me?" he asked, a little breathless at the greeting.

"Mondays suck," Laurence said between kisses. "Missed you all day."

Josh's heart flipped at the words. "You too, baby," he said against Laurence's throat.

Laurence rocked his head to the wall, offering himself and Josh ran with the invitation, nibbling and kissing to his heart's content. Burying himself into the crook of Laurence's neck, he drew a deep lungful and sighed. "So good," Josh murmured against the smoothness. He couldn't keep his hands off the other man. Laurence wasn't helping, digging his fingers into Josh's hair and hanging on, keeping him pinned lips to skin. Undulating shivers rolled down his captured body.

"I stopped by the store on the way home," Josh said. He stood straight, holding Laurence secure.

"Oh?" Blue eyes were slow to open, dazed and sexy.

Josh didn't elaborate, instead carrying his cargo through his apartment to the bedroom. He gently stretched Laurence out on the bed. "Tell me something, baby." He laid down beside him and wiggled a hand beneath Laurence's shirt to massage his abdomen.

"Sure." Laurence stretched then kicked off his shoes.

"Why the condoms for blowjobs? I know it's not a pregnancy issue here."

Laurence stared up at him for a moment, then his expression gentled. With a clearer gaze, he said, "It's for both our safety. Did you always wear a condom when you had sex with a woman?"

Josh pinched his lips together, but had to honestly shake his head.

"I've never gone bare with anyone, but I still get tested." Laurence threaded caring fingers upward again, easing the tension clouding Josh's thoughts away with massaging strength.

Josh didn't want to whine, but he hated everything about the taste and feel when he sucked off Laurence. "Can we change that?"

"That's a big commitment," Laurence whispered. His stroking hand faltered.

"Bigger than being monogamous?" he asked.

Laurence tilted his head. "Well, no. Not when you put it that way."

Josh heard the questioning hesitancy in his reply. "Buuut..."

"We've been together a week, Josh," Laurence explained with patience.

Josh's eyes closed and a shuddering breath, an aching exhale, slipped from him. He removed his hand from beneath Laurence's shirt. "You still think I'm living in some made up la-la land." These doubts were really beginning to wear him down.

Laurence growled. "No!" Laurence's fingers clenched in his hair, stopping any retreat. "I'm not. I *am* saying we can take our time." Laurence relaxed on the bed, ensuring Josh followed. When he was lying beside Laurence, an arm wrapped beneath Josh to hold him close, Laurence said, "This is new to me too, caveman."

"How?"

Laurence seemed to think something over before saying, "Promise not to laugh?"

"With you, never at you."

Laurence huffed a sharp chuckle. "You're my very first relationship."

"Seriously?" Josh hadn't expected that.

"As I can be," he returned. His fingers resumed their stroking through Josh's hair.

"But I thought... I mean, you did mention... Didn't you?" Josh reclaimed his spot under Laurence's shirt to stroke his abdomen as well.

"Fun. Nothing even remotely permanent. I didn't have boyfriends, I had dates."

"Why?"

"Honestly, because I liked being free. I hit college and crap, there were gorgeous men everywhere. Gay or straight, I looked. I didn't want a boyfriend getting pissy over that, getting jealous and possessive. I wasn't a slut, but I was a kid in a candy store for a while."

Josh nuzzled against his temple. "So why me? Why now?"

"Because you said it best. I *know* you and I do trust you." Laurence rolled to his side to gaze into Josh's eyes. "I liked you from the minute I met you before I realized you were straight as a two-by-four, then there was the whole confusion thing thinking you hated me. I learned how to deal with that, and probably started a few fights myself out of frustration, because you've always been able to get to me."

"I have?" Josh couldn't stifle the rush of pleasure at that admission.

"Don't let it go to your head." Laurence was quick with a stern warning. "So, if I want to take it slow, it's not because of you, but because of me." When he looked up again, the clarity of those blue windows shook Josh to his soul. "I don't want to hurt you, Josh."

"How about we make the effort to try not to hurt each other? There's some things that we can't control, but we can both try."

Before Laurence answered, Josh's phone rang. Laurence reached and planted a hot kiss on his mouth. "I will if you will," he breathed, swallowing hard.

"Then the rest will happen the way it's supposed to." He brought Laurence close for a softer claiming kiss. The phone stopped ringing before he wanted to let go.

A few minutes into their necking session, it started ringing again.

"Persistent shits," Josh groused. Laurence laughed beneath him, petting his chest.

"Just answer it already."

Reaching behind him, he faced the other way and palmed the phone. "Hello?"

"Hi Josh, it's me."

"Hey, Gregory. What's up?" Josh bit his lip when Laurence's hand slithered up his back where he lay twisted on the bed. He stifled the moan at the heat of lips to his shoulders. Laurence had lifted his shirt and was roaming.

"Mom and Dad are doing the end of term slaughter. You in?"

"Um... Uh, yeah, sure." God, he couldn't think when Laurence was doing that! "Are they— Are they coming to graduation?"

"Of course." There was a short contemplative quiet. "Josh, do you have company?"

"Actually, yeah." He bit off the urge to moan. Laurence's evil tongue was painting stripes of liquid fire up his spine.

"Dude! Say something next time." Gregory was laughing. "You sound like a nine-hundred number. Heavy breathing."

Josh groaned and laughed. "Sorry."

"Hey, if you see Laurence, see if he's coming. He hasn't been home much the last week. Can't find him."

"I can do that."

"Cool. See you Saturday." Then the line went silent.

"You are in so much trouble," he warned Laurence. He hung up the phone.

"Oh?"

Josh rolled over and pounced, catching a laughing Laurence. All that faked innocence, his *what did I do?* stare right up front. His eyes were sparkling like morning skies. Then Josh kissed him and that was all there was for quite a while.

CHAPTER TWENTY-THREE

GREGORY CLEARED his throat at the dinner table. "I'm moving."

"What?" Laurence tapped the side of his head with the heel of his hand. He knew he hadn't heard right. "You're leaving us?"

Gregory nodded, keeping his gaze averted. "Yeah. I need to go."

"What about your work?" Josh asked, equally stunned. "Thought you had two years."

"I've made an arrangement to do it freelance." Gregory's shoulders slumped.

"It's okay, honey," Mickie, Gregory's mother, said, patting his forearm at her side. "We're sorry to see you go but you have to get out in the world."

Laurence pouted. "He told you already?" Both Josh and RJ were as shocked at this bombshell of news as he was, all three searching the others around the table and none seeing anything different.

Ian shrugged, sitting straight to sip at his wine. "We all talked about it earlier this week. We are his parents," Ian teased trying to soften the blow for Laurence. Gregory's parents were as much their adoptive family as they could be. These dinners were a mainstay, and had been since the beginning of school between the four and Gregory's parents.

"Where are you going?" RJ asked, eating again.

"I'm looking at either Texas or New Mexico. Lower living expenses for someone like me just starting out."

"Wow," Laurence exclaimed. "When you say moving, you mean it."

Gregory looked up, sorrow and something more clouding his eyes. Whipping around to catch the other two dumbfounded stares at the table, he began to suspect the reason behind this was more than just trying something new, finding a new place.

Meeting Josh's gaze across from him, he shook his head once at Laurence, and just like that he knew what the cause behind this really was.

Rachel.

Somehow, she'd managed to hurt Gregory, again. Laurence leaned over, shoulder to shoulder and rocked him gently. "Just so long as you keep the couch open. You know the rule."

Gregory smiled, his first real attempt at one since making the announcement. "Always."

"Who's ready for more wine?" RJ held up his glass. "We need to toast our best friend on his next journey."

Laurence put on a brave smile and held his glass up. Soon, the atmosphere lightened as they began to chatter about other things. It just sucked because with graduation less than two weeks away, he knew he was going to miss Gregory like his own brother.

"SO, WHEN ARE you going to tell?"

Josh tilted his head in confusion toward RJ, sitting beside him at the dinner table. Ian and Mickie had left to let the four friends hang out like they usually did, but Josh was completely clueless to what RJ was asking about.

RJ yelped and jumped in his chair, glaring across at Laurence. "What was that for?" He bent and rubbed a shin.

Laurence scowled at RJ. "Zip it!"

"But—"

"I said leave it alone, RJ." Laurence scowled.

"What's going on?" Gregory leaned on his elbows on the table, curiosity edging his voice.

"Nothing," Laurence said for RJ, glowering at him.

Josh was completely lost, though the way Laurence was snapping at RJ wasn't making him feel too secure. It wasn't unusual for Laurence to sit beside Gregory. It had been the way of it since the beginning to keep Josh and Laurence the furthest apart. Changing that now would raise eyebrows, not to mention a few questions.

Somehow, RJ had figured it out. Josh tried to catch Laurence's gaze, but he wouldn't look toward Josh. Was he ashamed of being with him now? Didn't want their friends to know? Did he think it would be that much of a shock for them?

Sweeping his glass of water from palm to palm, he said, "I think there's something I should also tell you." He quickly looked up, just once, then dropped to stare at his water. "With graduation, things are going to change between us, and I know it. I want all of you to know I'm still your friend." He drew a shuddering breath. "I also want to apologize for anything I've done that has ever made any of you, anyone, believe I thought less of you."

"Josh."

He heard Laurence's quiet pleading, but didn't look in his direction. He wouldn't say anything about them being together. He wouldn't do that to Laurence without talking to him about it first. This wasn't about *them*, but here, this group should be where he could tell the truth and be accepted. He still hadn't told his family yet. He was leaving that for his trip later in the summer, when he would be going home for a visit. This was a test run. There was a measure of safety among his friends. Josh wasn't above using it. The flip and roll of his stomach was still there, but he knew it would be a lot worse when he finally sat down with his parents to tell them.

"It's taken me a long time to realize what I was fighting against." Firming his resolve, he sat straight not shying from what could possibly change everything or nothing. "I'm gay."

Gregory's mouth fell open. It was a shock his face didn't hit the table. "You're shitting me?"

"No."

RJ sputtered in clear disbelief. "It's true?"

Josh canted his head, questioning what he was talking about. *Was what true?* Then RJ was playing with his phone, evading a grabby Laurence from across the table by holding his phone out of reach.

Josh thought he was going to be sick when he saw what waited for him on the screen.

"You're full of shit, RJ," Laurence hissed, sounding like a pissed-off tom. "What happened to 'you'll get hurt' or 'he's not gay'?"

RJ slouched in his chair. "I was wrong, okay? Seriously. No man looks at another with that expression and doesn't feel it."

Josh's hands were numb. The phone and its picture were right in front of him now. There he was with a lap full of Laurence, both practically sucking the other's tongue down their throat. Then it hit him. He was at Club Six, sitting beside Sean and the boys. A week ago.

"You've known," he mumbled emotionlessly. Josh lifted from that damning picture, feeling his glare deepening as he fought to concentrate, and couldn't. All he saw in his vision was that one photo. "You knew." Then he whirled on Laurence. Laurence had known RJ had this and had never said anything to warn him. They'd *talked* about this, about Josh, about Club Six. About that photo. RJ and Laurence. He'd let Josh make a fool out of himself thinking he was protecting Laurence. Obviously there was no need for it.

"Did you tell him everything?" he challenged. Was this why he kept asking when Josh would feel comfortable coming out? Because Laurence had already told RJ? Josh couldn't look at Laurence, his hand clenched around the phone. Josh didn't want to know the answers.

Throwing the phone onto the table, he lurched out of his chair. Now Josh knew why Laurence tried to warn him. He really didn't want them to know Laurence was with Josh. Not by the way he reacted to that photo. What had he told RJ? His stomach rolled, curling up on itself. He had to get to out of there.

"Josh!"

He didn't slow down, stalking out the front door to reach his car. The car door slammed and he was gone.

"WHAT THE fuck, RJ?" Laurence snarled. He grabbed the phone and deleted the picture. "Couldn't you have left it alone?"

"I'm sorry, Laurence. I am," he replied, his head hanging.

"You pushed him."

"He's really gay?" Both he and RJ spun when Gregory spoke, having forgotten he was even sitting there in dumbfounded silence.

Laurence sank into his chair. "Can you forgive him for not saying anything? He never meant to hurt anyone." The man did deserve a chance to come to terms with something like this before springing it on his best friends, right?

"Forgive him?"

Sliding a savage glare toward RJ, Laurence clarified, "It happened the night we all went to Club Six. *We* happened."

That seemed to take a minute to sink in. Gregory gaped at them. "Wait. You and Josh?"

Laurence bit his lip and nodded. "Yeah."

"Why did the picture piss him off so bad?" RJ asked. RJ gave them the *I thought he knew* look.

Laurence growled impatiently. "Because I hadn't mentioned it to him. Any of it."

RJ crossed his arms. "So he didn't know you'd needed a sounding board and talked to me about this new Josh?"

Laurence blinked, fighting the pressure behind his eyes. "No." God, had he just fucked up everything?

"Shit." RJ raked a hand through his hair. "You can't hide things like this from him, Laurence. You should have told him you needed someone to talk to."

"Not my fault!" He leaped from his seat. "Christ. Now I have to find him. We'd barely talked about him coming out. It made him nervous."

"My news likely did it," Gregory said.

"And what's that all about?" Laurence demanded. "Why are you leaving us?"

"I need to get away." Gregory picked at something on the table. Something microscopic.

"Because..." Laurence prodded.

Gregory huffed. "Fine. Rachel is getting married."

Laurence put a caring hand on Gregory's shoulder. "Sweetie. You have to let her go."

"I have. I just want it to stop hurting," he mumbled forlornly. "I need some space. That's all. I'll be back."

Laurence turned to RJ. As much as he'd love to stay and help comfort Gregory, Josh needed him more. "RJ, I need your keys. I have to find him."

He handed over the key ring. "Bring it by in the morning. I'll get you home again."

"I'll call you," was all he said as he jogged from Mickie and Ian's. "Please, Josh," he whispered, but he honestly didn't know what he was asking for.

Driving the streets carefully, he managed to reach Josh's without incident. He let out a deep sigh when he found and parked right next to Josh's car. Dashing inside, he was up the stairs and pounding on his door in nothing flat.

"Josh! Open this door."

It burst open beneath his hard fist. "What?"

Laurence entered, with no idea how to fix what had happened. A stiff Josh stared at him, or really through him. "I'm sorry. I spoke to RJ the Monday after you kissed me. I was confused. For four years, you were straight."

Josh crossed his arms.

"I don't know who sent him the picture. Please, Josh."

"Please what? RJ already knew. It shocked Gregory, but you... You're the one who hurt me."

"Me?" he whispered, wringing his hands in front of him. "How?"

"I wasn't going to say anything about us because we hadn't talked about it, about letting anyone else know we're together. I thought you were getting comfortable with being a couple, us, because of Sean, because of our history.

Apparently, that only applied to people who weren't our friends pre-caveman, isn't it? You really didn't want them to know." Josh whirled away. "Is that why you want to 'take our time'. Are you waiting for some gay expiration that I don't know about?"

"That's low!" Laurence cried, following on Josh's heels when he smacked the door shut to spin away. He stomped deeper into the apartment.

"Is it?" Josh snarled. "Two weeks isn't all that long to be together, but Laurence, *we've* been *friends* for years. Doesn't that matter?"

"Of course it does!" He crowded up into Josh's space. "I was trying to keep RJ from pushing you into saying more than you were ready for, not to rush you, not because I didn't want them to know about us. I don't care if the world knows, but I don't want you to do something that will be uncomfortable for you."

When Josh sank to the edge of the bed, Laurence went with him, thigh to thigh. He placed a light hand on the leg closest to him. "I know this hasn't been easy for you. I— Josh, I love you."

Josh covered his hand with one of his. "I love you too," he choked out.

"I guess this falls under the 'try not to hurt you' umbrella." Laurence rested his head on Josh's shoulder. "I didn't mean to. I knew about the picture, but I didn't know he'd kept it, or that he'd whip it out at dinner tonight."

"Whip it out at dinner." Josh snorted hard.

Laurence rolled his eyes. "And there's my caveman."

"Am I?" he asked quietly a moment later.

"What?"

"Am I still your caveman?"

Laurence urged him close and nibbled at his bottom lip. "Josh. Let me say it again in case you didn't catch it the first time. I. Love. You." He sighed happily when Josh reciprocated, playfully snagging at his lips. A knock at the front door broke them apart. "Expecting someone?"

Josh looked just as confused. "No." Standing, hand in hand, they left the bedroom for the front door.

Gregory was waiting there when Josh opened it.

"It's safe, RJ. There's no blood," he said over his shoulder. "Have you made up?"

"We were getting there," Josh stated.

"Good." He walked in, not waiting for Josh to make way or invite them in. RJ trailed, looking far guiltier than when Laurence had hotfooted it after Josh. RJ shut the door.

"Now explain this to me, from the top please." Gregory sat down on the couch and crossed his arms.

"I told him tomorrow would be better," RJ interjected, avoiding both Laurence and Josh to sit quietly.

"Tomorrow, one of them could have been dead."

Josh and Laurence shared a quiet laugh, shaking their heads.

Josh sat down and when Laurence went to sit on the couch, Josh captured Laurence and tugged him down to Josh's waiting lap. With a contented sigh, he curled up in his favorite spot and let the story begin.

ABOUT THE AUTHOR

Diana DeRicci is the sexy, flirty pen name of Diana Castilleja. A romance author at heart, DeRicci's writing takes you into a saucier spectrum of sensuality and sexual adventure, where a happily-ever-after is still the key to any story. Diana lives in Central Texas with her husband, one son and a feisty little Chihuahua named Rascal. You can catch the latest news on all of Diana DeRicci's writing and books on her website Listed above. Feel free to drop Diana an email. She'd love to hear from you.

Visit her online at www.dianadericci.com

PURPLE SWORD PUBLICATIONS
www.purplesword.com